DEATH HANDED DOWN

DEATH HANDED DOWN

A Mags O'Malley Mystery

Kathleen Breen

ISBN: 978-0-578-97504-7 (paperback)

Dedication

Dedicated to my dear friend Missy—Mary McLaughlin Bartlett—without whom Maggie O'Malley would never have seen the light of day. Missy's persistent encouragement, her willingness to read and re-read—whether in the failing light of the front porch or over Zoom—and her remarkable patience with my impatience all make this book as much hers as mine.

Table of Contents

Acknowledgements

I want to thank my children, Celeste Lagrotteria and Jonathan Santamassino, for telling me again and again that I am their favorite mother and that they believe in my ability to accomplish wonders. Their affection, sense of humor, and tendency to brag about me to their friends have always warmed my heart.

Thank you to Judith Rice for connecting me to Carol Butler of Butler Books. Carol's advice and moral support, in turn, led me to my editor Sarah Jane Herbener, whose assistance in shaping this manuscript improved it tenfold. The precision and sensitivity of her editing astounded me.

My gratitude also goes to David A. Casey, who for the fifteen months of Covid isolation encouraged me to keep writing. His willingness to listen to chapters in their various reincarnations and his knowledge of and interest in Lincoln kept me focused. Thanks also to Kathy L. Nichols of Farmington Historic Plantation for her assistance in verifying historical data and providing information on what is currently happening at Farmington.

~1~

Murder Most Foul

The last thing Maggie O'Malley expected when she and her brother Jack went to the opening night of Shakespeare in Central Park was to witness a murder, even though the play was *Hamlet.* The early June evening had only promised the long-awaited summer ritual of packing a picnic basket and finding the perfect spot under the lush canopy of oak and ginkgo trees.

Nearly a fourth of the population of Hagan's Crossing, Kentucky—a small town on the banks of the Ohio River—had turned out for the opening night, toting old quilts and cushions, carrying small coolers of picnic suppers, and settling in for the evening.

Throughout the summer season plays began in daylight, but as the sun set and Act One flowed seamlessly into Act Two, darkness would seep from the leaves and fireflies would emerge from the honeysuckle bushes that rimmed the amphitheater. The call and response of tree frogs would punctuate the actors' dialogue.

Mary Margaret O'Malley had grown up in Hagan's Crossing with an older brother, Jack, and a younger brother, Donald, who died at 17. Only 18 months apart in age, Maggie and Jack had grown closer in their adulthood. He was five feet ten, with a stocky build, blue eyes, and black hair, although the salt-and-pepper effect was taking over. Jack had been widowed two years earlier; he and his wife Linda had a daughter, Grace, and a 15-year-old granddaughter, Anna. Jack was eligible for retirement from his professorship in the art history department at McLaughlin College, but he wasn't ready to take it. Grace was a nurse practitioner in a family medicine practice in town. She had been widowed when her pilot husband was killed in Afghanistan when Anna, their only child, was six years old. Grace was very close to her dad, especially since her mother had died.

At 22, Maggie married Dennis Geraghty, her college sweetheart, but five years later Dennis died in a fall at Red River Gorge while on a hiking trip with college buddies. Maggie never made a conscious decision to stay single afterward, but later chances to remarry didn't pan out. Fifteen years after Dennis's death, she changed back to her maiden name. Maggie had loved Dennis, but she wanted to feel like an O'Malley again. Family heritage had become important to her, so much so that she spent her career working on genealogy and local history. Now in her early 60s, she freelanced as a genealogist and often wrote about the history of the Kentucky counties that bordered the Ohio River between Louisville and Cincinnati.

Jack swung his Mazda Miata into the gravel parking lot, spraying pebbles everywhere.

"I've never been so thankful for a seat belt in my life," Maggie said, giving him a playful punch on the arm. "You're having way too much fun with this new toy."

Jack laughed and took a faded quilt from the small trunk. It was a short uphill walk to the large octagonal pavilion that had been built next to the outdoor amphitheater for such purposes as this opening night reception. The pavilion was set within a grove of oak trees and had sliding glass doors that could be opened or closed according to the season. Also surrounding the amphitheater were tennis courts, concessions, and a large fountain.

Patterned after the Olmstead parks in New York and Louisville, Central Park lived up to its name, functioning as a site for summer Shakespeare plays, Oktoberfest celebrations, and a Winter Wonderland festival. Maggie remembered her father bringing her to see live reindeer here when she was seven.

"Oh, isn't this pretty? I love what the new scenic designer has done with this space." Maggie had taken an interest in the restoration of the park's amphitheater and had been rewarded with a seat on the board. Her gregarious nature served her well there.

"It's very impressive," Jack said. "And look at this wall of portraits of the characters: each one looks like an Isaac Oliver miniature. Now that's really clever."

"Remind me who Isaac Oliver was?"

"Jacobean painter, a kind of miniaturist painter to the stars."

Maggie glanced happily around the room, which was decorated as an Elizabethan hall with heraldic banners, a golden velvet throne, and a dais. Waiters dressed in doublets and hose moved among the guests, offering hors d'oeuvres and champagne. A lute player circulated too. Maggie recognized all but a few people.

"Oh no, quick, hide me," Maggie hissed. "Amanda Filcher is making a beeline this way, and I don't want to get caught hearing the story of her grandfather again." Amanda was Maggie's neighbor, a secretary to the police chief, and an inveterate talker.

Jack stepped to the left to block Amanda's view, but he was too late.

"Maggie!" Amanda swooped out of the crowd and fastened her hand on Maggie's arm. "I am so glad to see you here! I wanted to tell you that I took your advice and went to that library in Cincinnati but I didn't call ahead and they were closed so I'll have to go back again their website didn't have the correct hours on it and I was so aggravated but I guess that's the way it is I want to tell you all about my grandpa who was a justice of the peace I want to find the court records and—"

Amanda finally took a breath, and Maggie breathed a sigh of relief as Erik Swenson, the theater company's producing director, a tall, lean redhead in his mid-40s, stepped onto the podium and adjusted the microphone.

"Welcome, everyone, to the opening of our 42nd season of Shakespeare! We believe we have a fine production of *Hamlet,* which will run for three weeks, followed by *As You Like It* and *Henry V.* Please return for all our shows. Many of our board members are present, wearing name tags. I'm sure they want to meet you and hear your suggestions for keeping our lovely regional theater alive and flourishing. Thank you very much for coming, and enjoy the show!"

Erik accepted the polite applause that followed and merged into the crowd.

"Well-dressed strangers at eleven o'clock," Jack murmured. "They look important. You ought to go schmooze."

Maggie excused herself from Amanda and approached a woman in a white silk suit who was standing stiffly beside a thin, bearded man. He looked distracted, his eyes scanning the crowd. Extending her hand to the woman, Maggie introduced herself and said some words of welcome.

"Are you visiting from out of town? Somewhere else in the state?" she asked.

"Oh heavens, no," the woman blurted out. "Absolutely not. I'm from New York; I'm a consultant for the Consortium of the Humanities." She paused, and Maggie thought she heard a sniff of disdain. "For some ungodly reason, we are having our annual meeting here at your little college. Seeing this amateur play is supposed to be a cultural activity." She put verbal air quotes around "cultural," as if her sneering smile had not been pointed enough.

Maggie took another look at the white suit and wrinkled her nose: Chanel, at least $800 or $900. Suppressing her desire to spill champagne down the front of it, she turned to greet the man. He was more gracious in his response, saying that he was thrilled to be in this part of the country, where focus on the arts and history were both strong. Maggie noticed that White Silk raised her eyebrows at this comment, then sealed her thin lips into a forced smile.

The man introduced himself as Avery G. Prendergast from Ohio, a member of the Ephemera Society of America, who was also attending the consortium at McLaughlin College. He was a broker in 19th-century items and documents, and he'd spent the past three days trying to persuade consortium members that ephemera were essential to the study of the humanities.

Maggie picked up the cue and asked him several questions about his business as a broker, what kinds of items he dealt with, and how he found out about them. He explained that auction houses often contacted him when an estate sale involved historical documents.

"Also, I have an established network of individual clients," he said.

"And have you enjoyed your time in Hagan's Crossing?" Maggie asked, giving White Silk a sideways glance.

"Yes, and I've met some interesting people. Just Tuesday morning in the hotel lobby—I'm staying at the Carter House Hotel downtown—I had a nice long conversation with a local man about 19th-century ephemera. He became keenly interested when I told him I had been contacted by someone in town with documents to valuate. He asked lots of questions, but naturally I couldn't divulge the particulars because of client confidentiality."

"That is intriguing, Mr. Prendergast. In a small town, news like that would be viral," Maggie said. "What's the most interesting item you've handled?"

"Well, I'm keen on the 19th century, so letters and documents from the Civil War era have always fascinated me."

As he described the various items that had passed through his hands, including a copy of orders sent by Lincoln to Ulysses S. Grant, a number of letters written by soldiers going into battle, and some diary pages from Jefferson Davis, Maggie observed his appearance. He was wearing a beige linen suit with a pink shirt and bow tie and had a rakish sort of haircut. Not quite corporate, not quite academic.

As he talked, though, Maggie nodded appreciatively, watching the contempt flicker across White Silk's face. Wickedly, Maggie encouraged Mr. Prendergast to talk on and suppressed a smile at how his swelling enthusiasm seemed to deflate his companion.

The lights in the pavilion flickered, signaling that the play would begin soon, so Maggie and Jack moved to their reserved seats. A breeze whispered in the tall ginkgo trees framing the stage house, and courtly Renaissance music filtered through the sound system. The music faded to silence, and a sudden flourish of trumpets began the action. Two sentinels approached each other across the castle parapet high above the stage.

"Who's there?"

"Nay, answer me, stand and unfold yourself!"

"Long live the king!"

The first half of the play went smoothly enough. The Ghost stalked the stage in a regal manner, Hamlet brooded, and Rosencrantz and Guildenstern tripped over each other both physically and verbally. Intermission began just after Hamlet revealed his plan: "The play's the thing wherein I'll catch the conscience of the king."

Jack and Maggie stood, stretched, and walked toward the refreshments. Jimmy Callahan, the chief of police, called out loudly from two rows away, "Hey, Mags, Jack—hey, you two! I haven't seen you in forever!" Catching up with them, he gave Maggie a kiss on the cheek and shook Jack's hand.

"I've been staying out of trouble, Jimmy. No more hanging around the pool halls."

Jimmy laughed at this, one of their old jokes, since Jack and Jimmy had both been headed for juvenile delinquency in their teen years and had escaped by the skin of their teeth. Maggie remembered her high school crush on her big brother's best friend, and looking at them together, she thought how well both of them had aged. She appreciated that now she and Jimmy were good friends.

Out of the corner of her eye, Maggie saw Jack's daughter Grace walking toward them with three glasses of wine.

"I knew you'd never make it to the concession stand, so I brought you these," she said, handing each a glass. Jack kissed Grace on the forehead and Maggie put an arm around her and gave her a squeeze.

"Hi, Chief Callahan. I didn't mean to interrupt."

"Oh, you're not, honey. I'm just gonna scoot to get a bottle of water before the play starts again." Jimmy Callahan hurried away, and Jack gave Grace a real hug.

"Anna's beside herself, isn't she?" he asked. "She called me to make sure Gramps was coming to see her stage debut."

"Oh, please, just get me through this night!" Grace said. "That girl is a bundle of nerves dipped in hormones. If we had one fight today, we had ten. She couldn't find the right shoes—her lime-green Chuck Taylors—and of course it was my fault because I'd had the audacity to put them in her closet. She said her hair was a disaster, and I insulted her by saying it looked perfectly fine—and then, since everything I say is wrong anyway, I agreed it was a disaster and said we should call in FEMA. That earned me a slammed door. By the time we got here, though, she was all smiles again. Her big scene is coming up, when she has to pantomime crying over the dead king."

"Well, come sit next to us for the second half and we'll cheer her on together," Maggie said. "Let me just pop backstage first and say, 'Break a leg.'"

She was gone for only a few minutes. The play began again and proceeded as expected. Hamlet bemoaned the "slings and arrows of outrageous fortune" and dispatched Ophelia, saying, "Get thee to a nunnery." Then came Anna's big moment. In the "dumb show," the Player King and Queen, both in masks, and Anna, as a motley jester with a mock scepter, seemed to glide onstage. The Queen mimed affection for the King and he for her. The jester made fun by blowing air kisses.

Then the Player King, feigning sleepiness, lay on the ground. The Queen left the stage, and Anna stood to the side, closing her eyes and tilting her head as if asleep. From stage left, a figure all in black, wearing a black mask, crept up to the King and poured a liquid into his ear, then fled the stage. The Player King cried out and tried to sit up but collapsed.

Seemingly startled by the cry, Anna opened her eyes and looked over at him. He had rolled onto his back and was twitching violently. Maggie had been startled too, and now she was alarmed. Was this an actor's flourish, or was something wrong?

A moment later, she got her answer when Anna, sagging in horror against the heavy tapestry backdrop, began screaming. Within moments, the house lights went up, the stage manager, the police chief, and Erik Swenson had all rushed onto the stage, and Grace had pushed past the crowd to grab her shaking daughter.

Chief Callahan knelt next to the body of the Player King, who now lay still. He felt for a pulse. After a moment, he looked up at Erik.

"We need an ambulance right away."

2

The Rest Is Silence

The chief asked for a microphone and stood to address the audience.

"Folks, we've got a situation here—this man is ill, and obviously we need to pause the play to take care of him. Could I ask you, please, to remain in your seats?"

Even as he was speaking, Maggie noticed, some people at the back of the amphitheater were starting to leave. "Damn," the chief muttered under his breath.

The next 12 minutes seemed interminable. Finally Maggie saw the flashing lights of multiple police cars and an ambulance wending their way through the park. As the blaring sirens grew louder, she felt mesmerized by the dizzying red and blue patterns on the treetops and the faces of the stunned crowd.

"What in the world just happened?" she wondered aloud.

Looking equally amazed, Jack answered, "Not exactly what Shakespeare wrote."

Now time seemed to stand still. The sirens had stopped, but the flashing lights, all out of sync with one another, continued. It was all happening so fast, though Maggie would later recall the scene in slow motion.

Maggie glanced down at her program. It identified the

Player King as Jesse Gilemorane, just graduated from Baldwin College in Ohio and making his theater debut. He said he was pleased to return to his Kentucky roots. Maggie recognized the actor's first name because Anna had a crush on him. He was seven years older than she was, and Grace and Anna had clashed over Anna wanting to hang out with him after rehearsals.

The chief made another appeal for the audience to stay, saying they needed to give the police their contact information. Officers began circulating in the remaining crowd, gathering names and phone numbers. The members of the acting company, plus Maggie, Jack, Grace, Anna, and the parents of other apprentices, sat waiting on the benches at the foot of the stage.

When the paramedics loosened the fabric around the actor's neck and removed the mask from his face, there was another shock. Erik gasped and uttered a curse word.

"That isn't Jesse Gilemorane," he said. "That's Ron Spear."

"Who's Ron Spear?" Callahan asked.

"Another member of the intern company. One of the Players."

Erik became distraught.

"Oh God, Oh God, I don't understand. There wasn't supposed to be anything in the vial. Pouring the poison into the king's ear was pantomime. And why was it Ron? Where's Jesse?"

"Erik, are you saying this isn't the man who was supposed to be the Player King? Why was he appearing in that actor's place?"

"I don't know, I just don't know. I was at the reception

while the actors were getting into costume. Elise, the stage manager, should know."

Erik gestured toward a young woman, who stepped forward.

"Elise?" Callahan prompted her.

Elise said Jesse had been on time for the call and the warm-ups and that when she'd seen the Player King in costume, she'd assumed it was Jesse. He and Ron were the same height and build.

"I saw Jesse park his bike when he arrived," she said. Heads turned toward the bike rack at the left of the stage. There was no bike.

"If Jesse came on time and left early, would Ron have taken his place without you knowing?" Callahan asked.

"I can't believe this; it doesn't make sense," Erik said. He put his face in his hands. "It is true that the actors in the play within the play experimented with changing roles. Ron wasn't otherwise in the pantomime, so if Jesse wasn't in place at intermission, Ron could have just put on the costume. He should have told Elise or me, but it was a little chaotic—you know, opening night. Or maybe Jesse asked Ron to take his place at the last minute."

He collapsed into a sitting position on a front bench.

Paramedics were unsuccessful in reviving the young actor. The medical examiner's forensics team arrived and cordoned off the whole stage house area as a potential crime scene. Yellow tape encircled the stage, the dressing room trailers, the props tables, and the scene shop trailers. They took photos, and the ME examined, then covered, the body. Crime scene investigators sprayed the area with luminol to look for traces of blood and then scraped a wet substance from the stage. Maggie watched with intense interest, feeling the urge to figure out exactly what had happened.

Callahan turned to interrogate the interns and apprentices who were cast as Players. They were all terrified.

No, they had not seen Ron putting on the costume of the Player King. Yes, Jesse was there for warm-up. They thought he had put on the King's costume. Didn't notice anything odd. No one had seen the man in black before he came onstage, but come to think of it, he hadn't been wearing Austin's costume.

"Austin?" Callahan asked.

"The person meant to play the poisoner in the mimed part of the play was Austin Wilke," Elise said. She looked around. "But he's not here."

"Well, we need to find Austin," Callahan said. "Where are the dressing rooms?"

Elise said that in addition to the two dressing trailers, there were public restrooms belonging to the park and also a couple of portables, several places where someone might have changed clothes.

"Or . . ." She paused. "He—or she—might have come to the park in that basic black outfit and blended in with the audience beforehand. It was just getting dark when we got to act three, scene two. Backstage is barely lit, so he could have slipped in through the trees."

Just then a uniformed officer approached from backstage, leading a thin young man dressed all in black, who appeared to stumble a little as he walked.

The officer said, "Chief, I found this guy in a porta-potty behind the dressing trailers. He was bound and gagged. Says he was hit on the head."

Erik rushed forward. “Austin, are you all right? Who did this?”

Haltingly, Austin said, “I dunno. I was just standing by the tree, stage right, waiting, and felt something hit the back of my head. I didn’t see anybody. I woke up in the dark and couldn’t move. I tried to kick the door open but I couldn’t.”

Callahan instructed the officer to take the young man to the hospital and stay with him.

“We need to know if Jesse asked Ron to take his place and exactly when and why he left. We need to locate Jesse Gilemorane,” Callahan said. “He could be in danger.”

“He’s staying with Miss Babcock on Woodbine Avenue,” Anna volunteered.

Callahan turned to Maggie.

“You know Miss Babcock, don’t you?”

Maggie nodded yes.

“How old is she?”

“In her mid-to-late 80s,” Maggie said.

“Well, we’d better check on her.” Callahan gestured to another officer and instructed him to go and ask for Gilemorane without distressing the elderly woman.

“Ask her if you can check the house—attic to cellar—but don’t frighten her, understand?”

Officers searched the area where Austin Wilke was knocked out and the route to the porta-potty. Even with the house lights fully illuminated, it was too dark to gather anything useful. While technicians bagged the body and placed it in the ambulance, the medical examiner told Callahan he would do a postmortem in the morning. They stood whispering for a few minutes, then the forensics team left.

Once again, Callahan took the stage. “Any idea who the

man in black was? Did he look like anyone in the company? Are you sure no one saw him get into costume?"

Maggie looked around at the assembled group, some just staring at the ground, some leaning on one another, some looking exhausted or worried. No one said a word.

Callahan directed everyone to go home. He stood for a few minutes with Jack and Maggie, rubbing his head worriedly.

"This is a puzzle. If they don't find Jesse at Miss Babcock's house, I'll need to put out an APB. I sure hope that kid Ron had an allergy attack or something. Whaddya think, Mags? You were sitting closer to the stage."

"What I noticed was how sudden and violent his twitching was. At first I thought he was overacting being poisoned, but then I saw he was in real distress."

The three of them were quiet.

"Well, nothing more we can do tonight," Callahan said. "It's too dark to search the park, and my officers have taken contact information from everyone who would stay. That's the problem with an open-air venue: no way to seal off the building. I'll have to get on it first thing in the morning. Everybody go home and get some sleep."

Ay, there's the rub, Maggie thought.

3

What's Done is Done

Maggie woke to the sun streaming in and realized she had not set an alarm. She remembered the night before and pulled the comforter up to her neck. It was surreal—the image of the Player King—a young actor from Tennessee pretending to be an itinerant Danish actor pretending to be the King of Denmark—in spasms and in the very real throes of death. It was really a play within a play within a play, she thought.

She watched the morning sun push shadows slowly across the opposite wall. She hadn't gone to bed until nearly 4:00 a.m., and now she didn't want to move at all. Her thoughts turned to Jesse, the kid who was missing, and she wondered why he had left the park. Pulling the covers over her head, she thought of her visit backstage during intermission. "It was about this dark," she said aloud. "What did I see in the gloom? I saw Anna and hugged her, and I complimented Hamlet."

Maggie closed her eyes and let the scene rise before her. The men's trailer, the women's trailer, and beyond them, the porta-potties. Closer to the back of the stage house, the long props table. An actor in the open doorway of a trailer and the stage manager talking on her headset. Something had struck her as off-kilter just before she had seen Anna—but what was it?

Remembering Anna, Maggie decided she should get up and check on her niece, then drive to the park. She told herself that as a board member she ought to be helpful in solving this mystery.

"Mary Margaret, be honest with yourself. You just want to dig around in other peoples' family secrets," she said aloud. She couldn't help laughing at herself. "Of course I do," she responded. "I am an O'Malley through and through. Right, Mama?"

It had been her mother's admonition all her life. "Maggie—you are *such* an O'Malley—just like your father—everything you know, you have to tell someone. Those people! Everyone in that family knew everybody else's business!" And the corollary, according to her mother, was that an O'Malley could never leave well enough alone.

The phone rang. It was Danny Baldwin: a veterinarian, a friend, a sort-of boyfriend. He was a widower, currently hosting a visit from his adult daughter, who decidedly did not approve of his seeing Maggie.

"Mags, are you okay? Do you want me to come over? I just heard what happened. It must have been terrifying. I would feel much better to have a look at you and give you a hug. Or you could come over here."

"I'm fine, Danny. Don't worry. I'm even taking it easy—still lying in bed—and I might stay here all day!" Maggie didn't mean this, but she wanted to ease Dan's mind . . . and avoid having to see his daughter.

"I'd be only too happy to come give you a back rub. Doesn't that sound inviting, Mags?"

Maggie laughed, assuring Danny repeatedly that she was fine and would see him soon. The phone call, however, prompted her to get up and get dressed. She had work to do.

Making coffee, Maggie checked her messages: one from Grace, one from her high school friend Mary Lou Johnson, and three missed calls from Franny Babcock. That was odd. It had been at least six months since she had last seen Franny, when she ran into the elderly woman at Danny's office. Franny was waiting with her dog Cecil and greeted Maggie loudly, to the amusement of other pet owners.

Maggie recalled how effusively Franny had declared herself Maggie's mother's oldest, dearest friend from school days. Clutching Maggie's forearm, she had recounted several stories of little Mary Margaret and Jack running through the neighborhood, getting into such mischief. Why, the two of them certainly were scamps and never turned down chocolate chip cookies fresh from the oven! Franny expressed her delight, her absolute delight in seeing Mary Margaret again and insisted that she come visit for a good, long talk. Only the vet assistant's announcement of Miss Babcock's name had allowed Maggie to say her goodbyes.

Was that the last time she had seen Franny? No—she remembered that a few days after that meeting she had overheard Franny in the crowded post office announcing the great discovery she had made of valuable papers in her attic.

"You'll be amazed at the treasure trove I inherited," Franny told the women around her. "Cleaning out my attic, my handyman found two enormous trunks that belonged to my great-granddaddy Isaac Caldwell and before that to his daddy, who was also named Isaac. They were both lawyers in Louisville. Great-Great-Granddaddy began in the 1830s, and he represented lots of prominent people."

She had gone on to explain connections in the documents between the explorers Lewis and Clark and the Kentucky Derby, how Clark's son had married a Churchill and their grandson had built the track. She boasted that everybody who was anybody was represented by the law firm. "I'm just sure there's something valuable in there!"

Maggie wondered if the police had found Jesse at Franny's—and if Franny had called her so many times because the police had frightened her.

Pouring herself more coffee, Maggie returned Grace's call to see how Anna was doing. The news wasn't good. Anna hadn't slept well and could barely stop sobbing. Maggie agreed to visit later in the day, if for no other reason than to give Grace a break.

Then she called Jack to see how he had slept. She suggested that Jack might look in on Grace and Anna and maybe take Anna for some ice cream later.

"She could use some grandpa love."

Maggie—or Mags, as her father had christened her in childhood—turned her attention to the cats who were sprawled across the sofa in the sunroom, lying atop a pile of photographs left there the day before. Although from the same litter, the two looked nothing alike. Maggie surmised that Finn and Fiona's mother had been a cat with loose morals.

Finn McCool was a husky orange long-hair with a mane like a lion and little tufts of fur between his claws. His golden eyes opened slightly when Maggie came into the room, and he stretched out to his full length. His sister, Fiona O'Malley, had short hair and an odd pattern of black and white markings that made her look like a Holstein. She had a sweet round face, green eyes, and a black beauty spot on her right cheek. Oblivious to Maggie, Fiona was washing her face.

Of the two, Fiona was far more inquisitive and stubborn. If Maggie opened a drawer, Fiona was in it immediately, poking her head into the corners. If Maggie moved her from a chosen spot, Fiona would defiantly return.

Now both cats had laid claim to the photographs.

Sitting on the floor next to the sofa, Maggie began stroking Finn's long, thick fur.

"Finn, where did Jesse Gilemorane disappear to during the play? And if he came from Ohio for Shakespeare, how did he end up staying at Franny's?"

Finn purred.

"Of course you aren't going to tell me."

Maggie looked at the pile of photos the cats had spread around. She picked up one black and white picture that had fallen beside the sofa. It was square, probably taken on an old Brownie box camera. Her parents, brother Jack, and a shy-looking five-year-old Mags gazed back at her from the grainy past.

They were on the front porch of the old house, across the street from Miss Babcock's. Maggie's dad had lifted her onto the coping and stood with his arms around her middle. She smiled, remembering the day the photo was taken. Instinctively, she reached down to touch her waist as if to feel where his hand had lain.

Nostalgia flowed into a wave of sadness as Maggie remembered the scene of Ron Spear's death the night before. If the acting company were a puzzle and Ron and Jesse were pieces, how did they fit together?

Maggie couldn't recall any Gilemoranes in the area, so had Jesse been referring to maternal relatives in his program bio? He'd said he was returning to his roots. He had gone to college in Ohio, but did he come from there? Erik Swenson could probably tell her something; after six weeks of rehearsals, Erik must have learned basic information. First, though, she would call Jimmy Callahan.

Amanda Filcher answered the phone with her usual emphasis: "Hagan's Crossing *Po*-lice."

"Hi, Amanda, this is Maggie O'Malley. Is Jimmy available, by any chance?"

"Naw, honey, he was in here this morning and out again like a hot knife through butter just don't know when he'll be back isn't it awful what happened at the play last night? I could hardly believe it you know—" Amanda always spoke in run-on sentences, making it hard to interrupt.

"Yes, yes, it is awful, Amanda. I'm sorry, but I don't have time to talk right now," Maggie said, hanging up rather too abruptly.

Her call to Erik Swenson was more successful. After they exchanged expressions of disbelief, Maggie asked if Jesse had been found. Erik said no.

"What do you know about him?" she asked.

"I just finished telling all that to Chief Callahan—again. He questioned me last night and for an hour this morning about every last detail: the actors, the rehearsals, the company finances, my 'movements,' as he called them. I'm starting to feel like a suspect."

"It's just his job." Maggie steered him back to the question about Jesse. She felt she ought to justify her interest, so she added, "I'm hoping that with my research skills I can help the chief."

Erik rehashed his biography of Jesse: raised in northeastern Ohio; parents deceased; might have been an only child; no mention of specific relatives or emergency contact; said he had discovered audition information on the internet and decided here would be a good place to start a career. Some of his mother's people had come from around here—a while back. A nice kid; cooperative, but a so-so actor; gave you the impression he thought he'd gotten a raw deal along the way. No, not really a chip on his shoulder, just an unspoken "I want what's coming to me."

"Don't the intern actors usually live in the same place, an extended-stay motel?" Maggie asked.

"Yeah, we have an arrangement with the motel that used to be an Admiral Benbow. But Jesse only stayed there two weeks. Then he moved to a room on Woodbine, with Miss Babcock. He was helping her with some family papers."

"Oh." Maggie paused. "I see. Okay, thanks, Erik—hey, how long do you think it will be before you restart the season?"

"That depends on the police, I guess. And I'll need two actors for Ron's and Jesse's roles." He paused. "This is just too much to believe—it's heartbreaking to lose a kid like that. And who knows what's happened to Jesse?"

Maggie thanked him and hung up the phone. She sat for a few pensive minutes before confiding to the cats that she was going over to the park to take a look around. "No need to share that with anyone, guys," she said.

Maggie always talked to the cats as though they were fully involved in everything. Giving them their own imaginary lives was a game she had picked up from her mother.

When Mags was about eight, her mother had named the family cat "Senator George Fulbright," and she'd regularly commented when George was missing for a week or so that "George must have gone up to Washington." Mrs. O'Malley had delighted in the pretense that George was the brother of J. William Fulbright, a prominent Democrat from Arkansas. When George would reappear at the back door, Maggie's mother would greet him with canned food and commentary on recent congressional affairs.

Maggie changed the cats' water and refreshed their food bowls. Finn was obviously hungry, and Maggie gave him a quick rub on the head. "Okay, I'm going," she told him. But before she got to the sunroom door, she stopped.

First, she thought, *I need to make another call.*

—4—

And Thereby Hangs a Tale

Franny answered the phone on the fourth ring, sounding somewhat out of breath.

"Franny, it's Maggie. Are you okay?"

"Yes, Mary Margaret, I am—I just rushed to get the phone. Honey, I'm sorry I called you so many times last night. I was being silly, I guess. But I was worried after the police came looking for that young man—he's a boy really—who's staying with me. I knew you were involved with the Shakespeare company, and I guess, well—"

She broke off, and Maggie could tell she was struggling for composure.

"No need to apologize, Franny. I'm just sorry I wasn't home when you called. I'll give you my cell phone number so you can reach me anytime." She paused. "Has Jesse come back? Have you heard from him?"

"No. No. I can't imagine where he is," Franny said.

Maggie urged Franny not to worry and changed the subject to her memories of growing up across the street from the Babcock house. Franny launched into the familiar narrative of Maggie and Jack as children. Maggie asked about

Franny's parents and grandparents, a question she knew would open the door to the discovery of the trunks in the attic. It had occurred to her that the man she met at the park might have been alluding to Franny's documents.

With very little prompting, Franny began to describe the items already found: a contract between the Churchill family and Meriwether Lewis Jr., related to the founding of the Jockey Club, the precursor to Churchill Downs; a letter from the actress Mary Anderson about donating land to the Franciscans in southern Indiana; and multiple documents related to Farmington, the plantation owned by the prominent and politically connected Speed family of Kentucky.

"Really? What kinds of documents?"

"Lists and descriptions of slaves, bills of sale, and runaway notices—quite a lot of correspondence connected to slavery. It's heartbreaking, really. Three generations of my family were lawyers representing branches of the Speed family. Of course, there is also a lot of random, unimportant paper, so it needs to be sorted through carefully." She paused. "That's why I advertised for help."

"Why did you pick Jesse, an actor?"

"Because he was so enthusiastic, I guess. Such a nice young man."

Maggie wondered if any of the Farmington papers would help her in completing the genealogy of Mary Lou, whose great-grandmother had been born enslaved there. Mary Lou was a childhood friend, and Maggie was happy to be helping her trace her family history.

"How long has Jesse been helping you?" Maggie asked.

"About a month," Franny said.

"Those papers might be interesting to historians. Have you thought about what you want to do with them?"

"I just thought that first I should get someone to sift through the mess and see if anything has real value."

Maggie suggested to Franny that she might come by later in the day—maybe bring lunch—and they could talk more about the papers.

"Maybe by then you will have heard from Jesse," Maggie added.

Franny's relief was evident in her voice. "Oh, thank you, Mary Margaret. I would be so grateful."

It was going to be a hot day, so Maggie put on light khaki slacks and a blue T-shirt. Looking in the bathroom mirror as she combed her short auburn hair, she noticed how the shirt seemed to brighten the blue of her eyes. She had the light complexion of the Flynn side of the family, but her skin wasn't as porcelain as her mother's. She sighed at the wrinkles she was acquiring and put on sunscreen and a touch of lipstick.

Her white Prius was in the drive. Getting in, she thought about Jack's new Miata and last night's white-knuckle ride to the park. On the way home, she had kidded him that they weren't in the Indy 500, and he had slowed down on the turns, preventing whiplash.

Now, reversing that route, Maggie drove through the tree-lined residential streets of town, past the high school, the elementary school, and several churches, to the business district about 12 blocks away. There she passed Mary Lou's café, the Cup 'n Saucer; the barbershop; Danny's vet clinic; and the courthouse. A red light stopped her next to the site of an infamous auction block and slave pen, now commemorated by a state historical marker. Maggie turned her head and a vision rose before her eyes:

> *It was a hot day. Forty or so African men, women, and children were crammed inside a wooden slave pen, surrounded by walls 15 feet high. One end was opened because an auction was beginning. A noisy crowd jeered and called out as a coarse man led a light-skinned woman to the block. He raised his voice above the noise, detailing her beauty, her ivory skin: "Why, she's only 1/64th Negro, ladies and gentlemen—see her fine teeth, in fact, her unquestionable value as a bargain at any price; imagine such an unspoiled female, and her only bein' sold to settle the debts of her deceased owner and father." A wealthy Frenchman had made a bid of $1,000, smugly assuming that he would win his prize, when a Methodist minister stepped forward to purchase the woman's freedom with $1,485. The woman fell into the arms of the minister, sobbing.*

Maggie knew the backstory of what she had just seen. The enslaved woman—a girl of 15, really—was being sold by her white half brother along with 30 others, many of whom were variously related to the slave owner. For years, the owner had raped the females of all ages, intending to "breed" field hands and house slaves. His reputation was widely known. When the old man finally died and his many debts had to be paid, an abolitionist congregation of Methodists organized a protest to the sale. The minister preached, "It is an evil to sell men and women like sheep, but it is an abomination to sell one's flesh and blood as if they were animals." He and members of his church had come to the sale with the money to buy the freedom of at least one person. This incident was memorable in the town's history because opposition to slavery had been rare.

Maggie's grandmother Nora, born in Ireland, was said to have had the Celtic "second sight," and, like it or not, Maggie had inherited it. The first time it happened to her, she was nine years old. It was early October, around dusk, and Maggie sat cross-legged on the front porch swing, singing to herself. Then, in front of her, she saw her grandmother standing at the far end of the porch. This was impossible, she knew, because Grandma was in a nursing home across town, recovering from a stroke. But there she stood, holding her hands out to Maggie with the most radiant smile. She said, "Goodbye, sweet, sweet Mags. I love you." Then she was gone. An hour later, the phone rang. The nursing home was calling to say that Nora O'Malley had been found deceased when they took supper in to her.

For years Maggie kept the secret, but when she had a second experience at age 12, she told her father about them both. She was crying and afraid he would say she was crazy. He listened without comment, then wrapped her in a big hug.

"It's a fearful gift, love," he said. "Time lets go o' you for a bit, and you're in the in-between. Your gran had it all her life. Don't be afraid. It can show you the past and the future, but it can't hurt you."

As she got older, every block of Hagan's Crossing gave Maggie a window into the past. She would look at a building and see its original rise in her mind's eye. Sometimes the history of a place felt visceral to her, as if she were wading into the past and the waters of memory were closing behind her. She never knew what might put her in this liminal space. She would hold her breath, standing for a few moments in two worlds at once, always surprised by the experience.

The light changed to green; the driver behind Maggie honked his horn in aggravation.

"Okay, okay, I'm going," she said aloud. "How long did I make you wait, buddy, two seconds? Geez."

She shook off the image of the slave auction and remembered Mary Lou's phone call.

"You need to call her, Maggie," she said aloud. "Don't forget, you made an appointment about the genealogy."

Talking to herself was a compulsion which she thought came from living alone for so long. Sometimes, in the car, Maggie would see someone in the next lane staring at her, and she would realize her mouth was moving. To hide her embarrassment, she would look down at the empty seat beside her and act as if there were a child the other driver couldn't see. Thankfully, she thought, more people were using Bluetooth phones in their cars now, and it wasn't so strange to see a driver talking out loud in an empty car.

Central Park was just south of the business district. Maggie pulled into a spot across the park from the amphitheater and walked toward the back of the stage house, scanning the ground for she didn't know what. Someone leaving the park after the intermission, not wanting to be seen, might have taken this route, and such a person might have dropped an identifying clue.

"Or not," Maggie said aloud, reaching the backstage area without seeing anything unusual.

Jimmy Callahan smiled slightly as she approached.

"Hey, Maggie, I expected you would show up here. How are you?" He rubbed his forehead with his left hand and extended his right hand to her.

She shook his hand. "I just thought I might be able to help."

A uniformed officer who had been talking to the chief frowned at Maggie.

"Just remember this is a police investigation, Ms. O'Malley," he said.

"Hello, Officer Kramer. I understand," she said. Callahan ignored Kramer, well aware that the officer didn't approve of his accepting Maggie's "help."

She turned to the chief. "What's next?"

"I wanna find out what happened to Spear. The ME is doing an autopsy right now, and he suspects an allergic reaction or a poisoning. Geez, I hope the kid was allergic to something he ate. Although that doesn't explain somebody shoving the Wilke kid in the porta-potty."

"I take it they didn't find Jesse at Miss Babcock's. Do you know anything more about him?"

"No. I hope I can find out something from Franny Babcock. I didn't know she was taking in lodgers. I wonder if that means she's having a hard time financially. I'm on my way to interview her now."

"Is there anything I can do, Jimmy?" Maggie ignored the glare from Officer Kramer.

"I guess you could look for Gilemorane families in your

genealogy stuff. That would be great." He paused. "Things like this don't happen in Hagan's Crossing."

"Yeah," Maggie said, "not lately, but the history of the town has some violent episodes. You'd be surprised."

5

WRIT IN REMEMBRANCE

Hagan's Crossing lay nestled on a bend in the Ohio River between Louisville and Cincinnati, on land that had been occupied by Shawnee hunter-gatherers until the mid-18th century. The gradual encroachment of white settlers—and the smallpox they brought with them—had eliminated most of the indigenous people from northern Kentucky by 1800.

James Harrod founded the first Kentucky settlement, Fort Harrod, in 1774, and one year later, Daniel Boone established Boonesboro. Following the Louisiana Purchase, the Ohio became an important waterway for western expansion; settlements developed along its 900-mile length from Pittsburgh, Pennsylvania, to Cairo, Illinois.

Moved by a spirit of adventure, Thomas Hagan—fresh from Ireland—came down the river in 1806 and stopped to build a ferry landing, which grew into a trading post, which grew into a town. With the ferry, he opened trade between Kentucky and Indiana, appealing to hunters and trappers from both sides of the river who wanted a market. When the steamboat flourished in the 1830s, so did Hagan's Crossing.

By 1860, the population of 1,200 included the congregations of three churches, Methodists, Baptists, and Catholics;

the inhabitants of large farms, producing tobacco, hemp, and corn for markets upriver; and a host of tradesmen, including a blacksmith, a cooper, a tanner, several seamstresses, a tailor, a grocer, a banker, and an innkeeper.

Now most of the town filled 20 square blocks set out in a grid pattern. Small farms dotted the outskirts, and thick woods sat between much of the town and the Ohio River.

Maggie considered Hagan's Crossing the ideal place to live. With a current population of about 4,000, it still felt like a small town; she had a wide circle of friends and acquaintances, and when she met someone new, they almost always discovered they had friends in common.

Maggie's great-grandparents had all come from Ireland in the famine years between 1845 and 1855. Not wanting to live in the tenements of New York, they had traveled west looking for farmland, which they found on the banks of the Ohio River. Two of her great-grandfathers had served in the Civil War, one as a provost guard in a Union prison camp in Louisville, the other as a paid substitute for an unwilling but wealthy draftee. Maggie often thought of the surprising confluence of events that had brought those eight individuals across the heaving Atlantic to find a refuge among these green hills—a landscape that no doubt reminded them of home.

Hagan's Crossing was a border town, not only between Kentucky and Indiana but between the South and the North. Technically, Kentucky had remained a neutral state in the Civil War, but Southern sympathies were strong.

The link to Indiana, however, was strong enough to make this part of Kentucky, including Louisville, as much midwestern as southern. Folks in Hagan's Crossing embraced both identities, their version of "y'all" having a hint of two syllables, more like "you-all."

Maggie had always loved to read, so her decision to become a librarian had been no surprise to anyone. To her mind, there were two places in the world where her sense of smell told her she was instantly at home: St. Boniface Church and nearly any library.

In the former, she loved the mixture of pure beeswax candles, century-old oak pews, and lingering incense. No other church had that precise scent.

Libraries, on the other hand, all evoked the same olfactory pleasure: the fragrance of collected books, ink on paper with hints of vanilla, almonds, and an underlying mustiness. Walking into a library, Maggie always stopped to breathe in the books. When she was young, she would escape the summer heat by going down into the stacks at the library, sitting on the floor, and pulling books to read at random. Hours would pass unnoticed until she would realize that she was going to be late for supper. She'd sprint home, slip in the back door, and be washing her hands by the time she heard her mother yell, "I told you, Jack, don't slam that screen!" Jack always got the blame.

Curiosity, interest in her own genealogy, and a love of libraries had also led Maggie to concentrate on research. For over 20 years, she'd headed the library's reference department, building a strong genealogy and local history collection. Occasionally she had been able to help people solve family mysteries, and it was that kind of digging for obscure information that raised goosebumps on her arms.

She could often sense when she was getting close to finding just the right property deed or marriage record. As when she was a child, Maggie could still lose all sense of time when she was doing research, but sometimes searching could also be tedious; in tracing her own family history, she had encountered 15 different spellings of O'Malley. Census takers had once recorded two brothers living next to each other, one with the name Malia and the other Malley.

Now that she was retired, Maggie still had a favorite nook in the library reference room where she could retreat with her laptop. At home, she couldn't get much done because the cats were both jealous of the computer. Finn could be sleeping soundly, but the moment she started to type—ever so quietly—he would jump onto the keyboard and lay claim to it. Or Fiona would lie on the desk next to Maggie and lay her head on Maggie's arm to immobilize it. It was much easier to work at the library.

Several months before, Maggie had solved a 75-year-old crime by tracing the genealogy of the wealthy victim and discovering a brother thought to have died at birth. As it turned out, the brother had been kidnapped as a newborn and raised to believe he had been an adopted orphan. When he discovered the truth and came to demand his inheritance, he accidentally killed his brother. Not revealing his true identity, he was acquitted by a hung jury—because no one could explain a possible motive. Digging through old records, Maggie had found a water-stained diary that unlocked the truth. That project was interesting, and Maggie was thrilled when it was written up in the local newspaper, the *Clarion*.

Maggie had a nose for uncovering information and hated to give up searching for an answer once she had begun. Now the death of Ron Spear had reached out and grabbed her friends and family, and there could be no turning away. Maggie decided she needed to do everything she could to get to the bottom of this, in part because she had witnessed the death and in part because her niece Anna had been traumatized by it.

-6-

And Nothing Is but What is Not

Franny Babcock sat rigidly on the burgundy camelback sofa in the front room of her home, a room which she still called the "parlor," as her mother had when she was a girl. Franny had grown up in the house and maintained the Victorian style of her great-grandmother, who, as the wife of a successful attorney, had spared no expense.

Franny herself might have been mistaken for a dowager of the 19th century, except that the dresses she wore were tea-length. Her iron-gray hair was gathered into a single braid that encircled her head like a crown, fastened with an antique silver comb. Her skin was remarkably smooth for a woman her age, and when complimented on it she always replied, "An ice-water wash in the morning and a sun hat in the garden!" This morning, however, she wore a worried expression and clutched a cotton handkerchief tightly in her hands.

"I just can't believe this, Chief Callahan. To think I took this young man into my home and now he's just disappeared. When an officer came last night to ask if Jesse was here, I couldn't understand what he was asking at first. He said there had been a death and they needed to locate the entire cast—and I couldn't figure out why the officer was here—I mean, Jesse would have been at the park—" Her voice broke, and she paused. Callahan waited silently.

"Do you really think Jesse is all right? I'm worried about him because he didn't come home at all . . ." She stopped again to regain her composure. "I was concerned when the officer wanted to walk through the house; he even went up into the attic. Did he think I was lying to him?"

Obviously trying not to cry, she looked down at her hands and untwisted the handkerchief, spreading it on her knee and tracing the embroidered initial *F* with one finger.

"No, Miss Babcock. The officer was just making sure your house was secure."

"Who was it again who died?"

"His name was Ron Spear; he was another member of the intern acting company. Twenty- three years old. It seems he just stepped in to take the role when Jesse wasn't in place."

Police Chief Jimmy Callahan felt ill at ease in the faded opulence of the room. He was a large man in his mid-60s, more muscle than fat. He had inadvertently chosen a chair too small for his frame, but the only other choices were to sit 18 feet across the room from Miss Babcock or to sit snugly beside her on the small sofa. As soon as he'd sat down, he'd regretted it. He couldn't have named the chair—a narrow bergère, upholstered in rose chintz—but its closed sides made him feel he had far too many elbows.

"It's ghastly," Miss Babcock said. "His poor parents. Is the young man from around here? I don't know any Spears."

"No, ma'am, he was from Tennessee. I had to call his parents and tell them on the phone. It's very sad."

The chief scooted a little to the edge of the chair and leaned forward as much as possible without tumbling over, but the marble edge of the low table in front of him dug into his knees. He grimaced. The room resembled the antique stores his wife had loved to explore when they'd taken car trips.

In one corner stood a grand piano with sheet music scattered across its tufted-velvet bench. Opposite, a large oak and marble fireplace with a wide, deep mantel dominated the wall. Every surface—the mantel, numerous small tables, and the top of the piano—was covered with framed photos, china figurines of women, porcelain angels and animals, crystal vases of roses and hydrangeas, and multiple Tiffany lamps. It overwhelmed him.

"I can't imagine what's happened," Miss Babcock said.

"Yes, ma'am, I understand. Could you tell me what you know about Jesse's family?"

"No."

"What?" He was taken aback.

"No, I don't know anything."

"He never mentioned any parents or siblings?"

"No, sir."

"Friends?"

"No."

"Did he say anything about where he grew up?"

"No." She shook her head sadly.

Callahan wrote the word "nada" in his notebook and underscored it twice in frustration. He shifted his weight and jammed his left knee further into the marble table, cursing inwardly.

"Tell me the story of how you met Jesse. Just everything you recall about the first time you talked and when he moved in."

"I suppose it was in February. In January I had sent a letter to several university newspapers, placing an ad asking for a part-time researcher or a kind of secretary to assist me. I also placed a notice at McLaughlin College here in town. I received three replies. Jesse first answered by mail, I think—or did he call me? I'm not sure about that because a couple of people called and somebody wrote. I did end up talking to all three of them. One was a woman who spoke in such a strong accent that I couldn't really understand her. Another, a man, wanted to charge me a small fortune; he seemed very condescending, and I didn't like him. Jesse told me he was going to be coming to Hagan's Crossing to perform with Shakespeare in the Park. I thought he must be smart to be doing Shakespeare."

Miss Babcock let out a little sound of surprise.

"Oh, Chief Callahan, where are my manners? I've let you sit here without offering you anything to drink. I have some iced tea—or lemonade, if you prefer."

She seemed genuinely upset with herself, and Callahan welcomed the chance to stand up, so he accepted.

"Iced tea would be fine, ma'am, but let me go with you to get it. You don't have to wait on me; we could continue talking in the kitchen."

She led him down a dimly lit hallway with oak flooring and high wainscoting into the kitchen.

"What is it that Jesse did for you, ma'am?" Callahan asked.

"He was going through a lot of papers that belonged to my granddaddy and my great- granddaddy. He was going to organize them and let me know what I have. I knew some of them might be valuable."

She poured a glass of tea. "It's unsweetened—I'm sorry,

maybe you prefer sweet tea? I suppose I could add some sugar, but it wouldn't be the same thing . . ."

"This is just fine, Miss Babcock. Thank you." He accepted the glass, took a gulp, and set it on the table. "Now, then, how long has Jesse been here?"

"At first he was living with some other actors, and I was paying him, but about six weeks ago, I offered him the room because it would give him more access to the trunks."

"Did he have expertise in old documents?"

"Well, he seemed to—he said he did—and he was very interested and spent hours poring over them."

"Did you say you paid him?"

"Only at first. When he moved in, I gave him room and board, but he kept irregular hours with the theater, and we didn't eat many meals together."

"Do you know if he had a bank account?"

"No, sir."

"Did he ever show you any identification? A driver's license, maybe?"

"No. He didn't have a car, just a bicycle."

"Did you get any references on him before you made this arrangement, Miss Babcock?"

"I didn't think to." She frowned. "I suppose that was foolish, but I thought the Shakespeare director must have trusted him. No, I just took him at his word."

"May I see his room, ma'am?"

She opened a door at the left.

"When the house was built in 1881, it's likely this was a bedroom for the cook. It has a nice view of the back garden and easy access to the kitchen," Miss Babcock said.

Plus access to the back door, Callahan thought. He turned

back to look at the spacious kitchen. "Did he have a key to this?" he asked, opening the door and stepping onto a wide veranda that wrapped around three sides of the house.

"Yes. He came and went as he pleased; mostly I didn't know when," Miss Babcock said. "My bedroom is in the middle of the house."

"When did you see him last?"

"Early yesterday afternoon. I came into the kitchen. His door was open, and he was putting things in his backpack."

"Did he usually take a backpack to the theater?"

"Yes."

"Did he seem anxious or worried?"

"He seemed to be in a hurry and didn't want to talk."

"May I look through his room now? I'm not sure how thorough the officer was last night. I'll come to the front room when I'm finished."

"Oh, yes, of course." She left him on his own.

Jimmy Callahan stood in the center of Jesse's corner room and examined each of the windows. The back window was open about an inch. It looked out onto a garden planted in a mixture of vegetables and flowers. Rows of bush beans were just coming up, and three tomato plants in cone-shaped cages made him think of small alien beings, with their green tendrils poking through the wires. Along the porch and the back fence, thickly blooming blue and purple hydrangeas clustered. He closed and locked the window.

In contrast to the clutter of the Victorian parlor, this small bedroom was sparsely furnished. A single bed covered in an old-fashioned chenille bedspread stood against the wall on the left, and at its foot a tall chifforobe with four drawers and a closet door filled the corner. He opened all the drawers—empty—and found in the closet a single white shirt dangling from a hanger. Putting on gloves, he took the shirt and folded it into an evidence bag he had carried in his inside pocket.

From the side window, Callahan could see the street at an oblique angle where it intersected with a one-way cross street. He sat on Jesse's bed and noticed a maroon Chevy parked on the cross street, Willow Lane. A man with dark hair and a baseball cap sat in the driver's seat reading a newspaper. Callahan tried to remember if the car had been there when he arrived; he wasn't sure. He closed the door and walked back to the front room.

"Did you find anything?" she asked eagerly.

"No, ma'am," he said. "I do have one more question, though: did Jesse ever receive any mail here?"

"No, I'm afraid not," she said, adding, "I haven't been any help to you at all."

"Oh, you've been fine, Miss Babcock. I know all this has been a shock to you; if you need anything, call me. Or if you remember anything, no matter how small."

Going out to his car, Callahan saw that the maroon Chevy was gone.

Genealogy of Franny Babcock

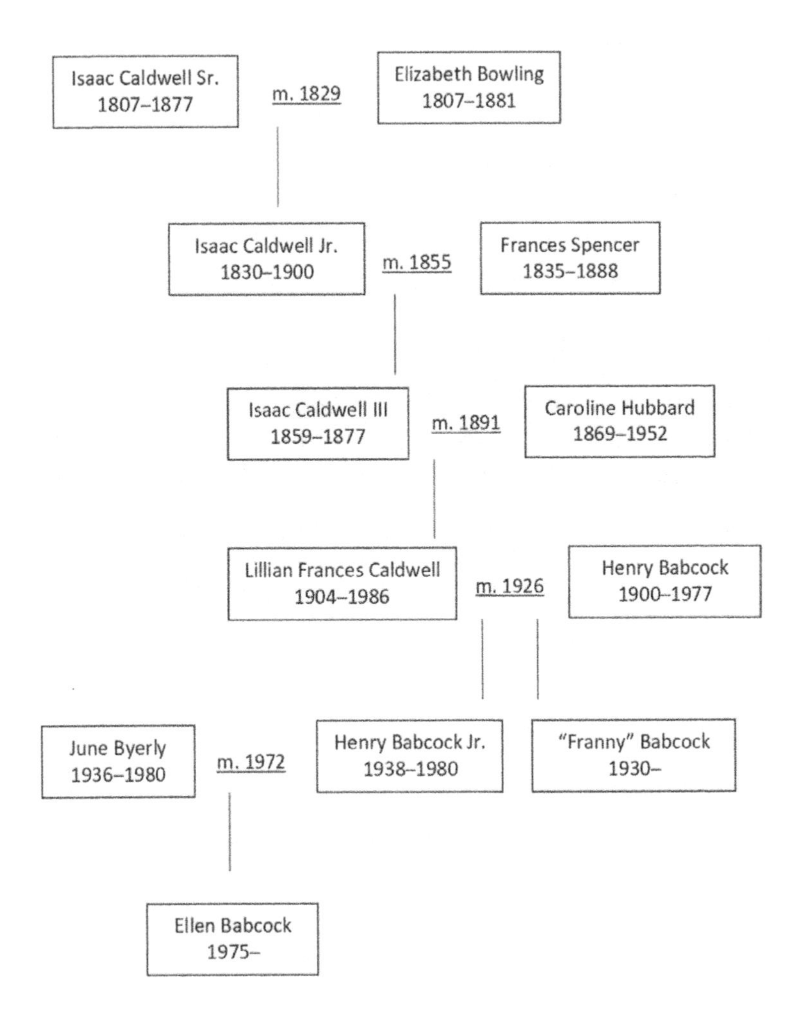

7

More Matter with Less Art

After leaving the park Maggie wanted a cup of coffee, so she swung by the Cup 'n Saucer and bought a newspaper at the stand by the door. Mary Lou wasn't in. She placed a luncheon order to go, then sat at a table by the window with her coffee in a to-go cup. The *Clarion* was a weekly paper that came out on Saturdays, so what she was reading was all old news. But she remembered that this issue had a preview on the opening of *Hamlet*, with lots of photographs taken of the cast in rehearsal at the park.

Between sips, she skimmed the story for any mention of specific cast members and examined each photograph closely. There was a grainy picture of the group of Players in costume, with an identifying caption, and it was uncanny how identical Jesse and Ron were in height and build. Maggie wondered if something had prompted Jesse to ask Ron to take his place in the pantomime scene. Maybe Anna could add something.

Taking the coffee and the packed lunch and tucking the paper under her arm, Maggie headed back to the Prius to drive to Grace's house, about five blocks south of the park.

She arrived to find her great-niece still cuddled up in her bed with two very threadbare stuffed animals: Napoleon, a bear, and Squeak, a raccoon. Napoleon—who, in recognition of his military battles, wore the uniform jacket of his namesake—was missing an eye and had his head bandaged in tattered gauze. Squeak's long striped tail, once fluffy but now stringy, revealed the years that Anna had spent clutching it, dragging him around wherever she went.

Maggie sat on the side of the bed. Anna scooted to a sitting position, hugging Napoleon in her lap.

"I'm so sorry, Anna, I'm so very sorry," Maggie said softly, rubbing Anna's back in a circular motion. "You're probably in shock, and it will take a while until you feel better."

Anna began crying. "Aunt Mags, please *don't* tell me everything will be better! It won't. The play is ruined, and Ronny is dead, and it was horrible. I opened my eyes and he was jerking and twitching, and I knew it was all wrong, but I couldn't move, and then I think I was just screaming—like I was hearing someone else screaming and realized it was me."

This poured out, punctuated by sobs, while Maggie wrapped her arms around Anna.

"And Ronny was so nice. He didn't think it was crazy for me to want to go to New York! Everything is ruined. And what happened to Jesse? He was nice too, and he walked me home sometimes, but Mom didn't like him." Anna paused and wiped her face. "Just don't tell me I'm overreacting and it will be all better!"

"No, it won't be all better tomorrow, but Erik may decide to open the show again in a couple of weeks, and he'll need you. You have to keep going; you can't quit."

"I know."

Maggie urged Anna to sit on the side of the bed next to her.

"It would help if you could recall everything that you saw and heard from the time you got to the park last night. I know Chief Callahan will want to speak to you at some point, but maybe you could just tell me what you remember while it's fresh in your mind." She saw a water bottle on the bedside table and handed it to Anna. "Here, you need this. Tell me what you remember."

Anna took a long swallow and a deep breath.

"Well, when I got to the park, I saw my friend Aiesha, who's an apprentice with the lighting designer. She was doing a check on all the wiring, looking for problems. We talked about how freaked out Elise, the stage manager, was, and then I went to the spot where all the actors gather to warm up. Everything was running late, so we were just standing around, waiting."

"Did you see Jesse?"

"Yeah—I saw him come up the incline on his bike and put it in the rack. He locked it and came over to the warm-up circle. Then, after the warm-up, I saw him backstage, looking out at the audience through one of the curtained entrances. He was standing really still, like he was watching someone in the crowd. I asked him what he was looking at. He said, 'That guy in the black windbreaker. I've seen him before, and he's . . . dangerous.' It was such a weird thing to say, and I wanted to ask why, but then somebody started talking to me, and I turned away from Jesse. I don't know what he did then."

"Do you remember anything else about who he was looking at?"

"No. The guy was toward the back of the house and a clump of people was blocking my view."

"Did anyone behave strangely, or did anything seem out of the ordinary, anything at all?"

"No."

"Did Jesse put on his costume?"

"I don't know. When I saw Ron offstage, I thought he was Jesse."

"You didn't notice that it was Ron wearing Jesse's costume?"

"No, they're"—she stopped—"they *were* the same size." Anna started to cry again, and Maggie gave her another hug.

"Thanks, hon," Maggie said. "That's very helpful."

Maggie stood, turned, and gave Anna a kiss on the top of her head. "I kiss you hade," she said. It was a family saying that went back to when her brother Jack was about three. His mother had told him she had a headache, so he'd climbed onto the couch where he could reach and kissed the top of her forehead, saying, "I kiss you hade." His mother, touched by the endearment, passed it on, keeping Jack's three-year-old pronunciation of "head"—and the whole family honored the gesture as the best comfort one could offer.

Maggie encouraged Anna to lie down again and tucked her in with another kiss. Then, going out to the kitchen, she sat a few minutes with Grace. Grace, too, had her grandmother's blue eyes and Cupid's-bow lips and the auburn hair that came from the Flynn side of the family.

"Gracie, you look worn out. Why don't you take a nap yourself? I'm pretty sure Anna is going to fall asleep again," Maggie said, stroking Grace's forearm.

"Maybe I will, Aunt Mags; I'm just glad this is my day off."

As they hugged, Grace added in a whisper, "Thanks."

Maggie swung by home to repack the luncheon foods into a large wicker picnic basket, adding table settings and napkins, much to the consternation of the cats, who thought they should be invited if there were chicken to be had.

After Chief Callahan had gone, Maggie pulled into Miss Babcock's driveway. Taking the basket from the seat beside her, she walked toward the porch. Franny, who was wearing a faded housedress, gardening gloves, and a floppy straw hat, came around the corner of the house.

"Oh heavens, Mary Margaret, I am so glad to see you! Again, I'm sorry about my long rambling messages about Jesse and the trunks. I don't want to be a bother—" Her voice broke a little, and Franny stood looking suddenly frail.

"I told you not to worry about phoning me, Franny. You need some TLC, so voilà!" Maggie held up the picnic basket.

"I called you so many times last evening, Mary Margaret, because I need to talk to you. I should have asked you about those papers in the first place, not that young boy. I'm so worried about him, and last night after the police came, I started wondering what I didn't know about him and whether I was foolish to take him in, and I got myself worked up in such a state as you wouldn't believe. Then, after Chief Callahan came to see me this morning, I was even more convinced I'd done the wrong thing."

Her eyes began to tear up. Maggie dropped the basket in the grass and took Franny in her arms.

"You must have been scared to death last night, here all alone. I'm sorry, Franny. I'm so sorry. This has been a shock." Franny took off her gloves, pulled a handkerchief from her pocket, and dabbed at her eyes. Maggie stood rubbing her hand up and down Franny's back.

"Everything will be okay, Franny."

"You are as sweet as your mama was, Mary Margaret, always thinking of ways to be kind. I am dreadfully worried about Jesse. The police chief had so many questions I couldn't answer. And he searched Jesse's room."

"Jimmy Callahan's a good man, and I'm sure he'll get to the bottom of this. Come on."

Maggie picked up the basket and led Franny up the steps to the glider on the front porch, then sat beside her.

"You can tell me about it."

Franny was recounting her conversation with Chief Callahan when she stopped abruptly. Maggie noticed she was startled and was trying to hide the reaction by smoothing her hair.

"What's wrong, Franny? What just happened?"

Maggie heard the fear in her voice. "It's that car, that dreadful red car that keeps coming through the neighborhood. I just saw him go through the intersection. Sometimes he slows down passing the house, and sometimes he parks and sits on the corner over there—just sits there in the car, sits there and watches or reads."

"What does he look like?"

"Usually he's wearing a ball cap. I don't see his face."

"How long has that been going on?" Maggie asked.

"Probably about ten days or two weeks. When I first saw him driving by several times, I thought he was a new neighbor, but then I saw the car parked over on the corner, with the same man sitting there every time. I don't know why he would be watching any of the houses around here, but I felt like he was watching, you know? I liked it when Jesse was here because I felt a little safer."

"Did you tell Chief Callahan about this?"

"Oh, no, he would think I'm just a crazy old woman who's watched too much television. I didn't even mention it to Jesse until several days ago."

"How did Jesse react? Did he seem concerned?"

"I don't know. I couldn't tell what he thought. He stood and stared for a minute, then—he just told me to be careful, not to worry. Do you think his disappearance has something to do with that car?"

"It's something to think about," Maggie said. She didn't want to add to Miss Babcock's worry, so she switched topics. "Would you like to have lunch around on the side porch? I've brought everything we need, even the napkins."

The Babcock house, the largest on the 500 block of Woodbine Avenue, was a typical Folk Victorian style, somewhat like a Queen Anne but with less ornamentation. Still, the wide wraparound porch was supported by turned spindles, and the corners were decorated with lacy spandrels that suggested the elegance of an earlier era. When Miss Babcock's grandfather had the house built, it was considered a showplace, and the family had always maintained the original Victorian colors, a light golden yellow trimmed in white.

"Let me go in and wash up first, Maggie," Franny said, putting her gardening gloves and sun hat on a side bench. While she was gone, Maggie went around to the side porch. She covered the round wicker table with a white cloth edged with blue hydrangeas, then laid out delicate cobalt- blue glass luncheon plates and crisp cotton napkins.

She had brought tarragon chicken salad, cheddar cheese biscuits, fresh strawberries and clotted cream, and iced tea. Maggie smiled at the effect of being transported to another time and place. "Or maybe just into the pages of *Southern Living*," she said aloud. At the squeak of the screen door, she brushed away some twigs from a seat cushion.

"Heavens to Betsy, Mary Margaret, this is too beautiful to eat! You went to far too much trouble."

"It was no trouble at all, Franny. I just thought we should take advantage of this delightful June day and enjoy ourselves with a touch of elegance. I just closed my eyes and imagined this shady porch, and the whole menu came to me in a flash." She didn't mention stopping by the Cup 'n Saucer to fill her basket.

They talked for a while about the food and the weather and Miss Babcock's memories of Maggie's mother. Then the conversation turned to Miss Babcock's grandfather and great- grandfather.

"My mama was born in this house, probably in the front bedroom. Before they moved here, they lived in Louisville."

"I know your family has a long history in Kentucky. The three generations who practiced law together were all born before the Civil War."

"Gracious, Mary Margaret, I forgot how smart you are about family history. You really should take a look at the papers," Miss Babcock said. "If you have time, I mean."

"Sure I do. Let's finish our strawberries, then I'll clear this and we'll go in."

They were quiet as they scooped up the last of the melting cream. Maggie scraped the plates and wiped them with paper towels, wrapping the whole collection of dishes in the tablecloth before placing the small bundle back into the wicker basket.

Franny led Maggie into a room with built-in oak bookcases lining three walls. Several large oak tables were covered with stacks of yellowed papers. On either side of a marble fireplace and mantel sat the two enormous trunks, both propped open and still more than three-fourths filled with documents on parchment, vellum, and fragile paper Maggie thought might be made from wood pulp or rags.

Franny pointed out some of the papers she thought might be valuable, then stood in the doorway for a few moments.

"You won't mind, will you, dear, if I go into the other room? I need to put my feet up for a while." Maggie agreed that was a good idea and turned her full attention to the work Jesse had done so far. It seemed he'd begun separating the documents according to purpose: one stack for wills, another for the filings of lawsuits, others for letters, deeds, depositions, interrogatories, summonses, and so on. Maggie realized what a big undertaking it would be to go through everything. Sitting in a leather chair befitting a Victorian library, she began to read through the stack of correspondence.

She was surprised that the first items she picked up were associated with Farmington and the Speeds: letters about the purchase and sale of various enslaved Africans, with a scattering of names: Phyllis, Morocco, Rose, Charles, and Frazier. However, there weren't as many names as there were inventories and descriptions of the human "property." She found an 1850 slave schedule that showed Philip Speed owned 15 people, beginning with "9 male black, 19 male black, 30 female black," as if age, gender, and color said all there was to value. On the same schedule, Joshua Fry Speed owned 19 people, several of them described as "mulatto."

Then she picked up a letter that really excited her. It was from Philip Speed to his attorney, seeking to negotiate the sale of a female, aged 27, named Athena Jackson. Maggie recognized the name. She knew from previous research with Freedmen's Bureau records at the National Archives that Athena had been her friend Mary Lou's great-grandmother. Here was corroboration of the work she had done, documenting that Athena was the mother of a mulatto child named Cassie Jackson and that both of them were enslaved by Philip Speed. She felt the hair rise on her arms in her excitement.

The letter didn't mention the sale of the child, Cassie, so it seemed that mother and daughter had been separated.

Maggie pulled out a handful of newspaper clippings offering rewards for the capture of "runaway slaves" from the Farmington and Oxmoor plantations. One signed by John Speed described the man, Charles Harrison, in great detail: "Rather a yellowish hue in the face, has fine slick skin, his eyes showing a great deal of the white and about 28 or 30 years old." It called him "a very intelligent fellow and remarkably handy," praising his skills in shoemaking, gardening, butchering, and bricklaying. It warned he might head to Indiana or Ohio or try to get passage on a steamboat.

She was struck by the discordant tone. The ad called him a "fellow" twice—a word which suggested friendliness—but promised $50 for the "apprehension and security" of him, "so that I can get him" if captured in Kentucky, and $100 if in another state. She felt repulsed by the pretended benevolence of the enslavers who thought themselves good masters and even claimed to be anti-slavery while buying and selling human beings.

Just then, Franny reappeared at the door.

"Franny, did you ever tell anyone else in town about the trunks and papers you found? Anybody at all, other than advertising for someone to help?" Maggie knew Franny had announced it to the post office, but she wanted to know if there were other times. She frowned at the thought of unscrupulous people who might want these trunks.

"Well, let me think. That was months ago; I know I was very excited about it, so I may have." She paused to think, then said, "You know, I did tell the members of my birders' group. We meet here once a month on Wednesdays, and I had just sent out the ads to the universities."

"Who are the club members? Were there a lot of people here? Do you remember anyone in particular?" Maggie asked.

"Only about seven or eight people come to the meetings regularly. The roster's in this desk drawer."

Miss Babcock turned to the desk by the door and took out the list.

"I guess Edie Miller, Tim Sandoval, Jeremiah Price, Lorene Spencer, Marshall Hardy, um, I'm not sure, probably Britt Taylor was there—oh, and Betty and Roger Craig."

"Did any of them show special interest in the papers?"

"Let's see, I mentioned that my great-great-granddaddy was a Louisville lawyer who represented a lot of prominent families and that I had found papers going back to the 1830s. I said some of the folks had unusual names."

"Like what? Do you remember specifics you mentioned?"

"Um, Peter Pirtle and Austin Peay. Somebody commented on the alliteration in 'Peter Pirtle.' Edie wondered if this Austin Peay was the namesake of the Tennessee university. And it seems somebody asked if I had seen the name of Speed—but I can't recall who. Why are you asking?"

"I'm just wondering who else in town knows about the papers. Did Jesse ever tell you he had found something unusual or rare?"

"No. Nothing more than the items I've mentioned."

A silence settled on the room for nearly a minute as both Maggie and Franny looked at the documents.

"Mary Margaret, I'm wondering if I could ask a tremendous favor of you." Franny looked very tired.

"Certainly. Are you all right, Franny?"

"Yes, dear, I am—but it worries me to have those papers here now. If I arranged for my handyman and his son to deliver them, would you mind taking the two trunks and all this"—she gestured toward the stacks of paper—"to your house?"

"Of course, Franny—anything to make you feel better." Maggie tried not to show on her face that she was doing somersaults in her head. She was thrilled to get her hands on the whole collection.

"Thank you, thank you, Mary Margaret. That makes me feel much better. Would it be okay if they brought the trunks over to your house tonight?"

"Absolutely!" Maggie said. "I don't want you worrying about these papers or anything, even about Jesse. The chief will find him."

Franny began describing a time when Jesse came in from rehearsal, reciting lines from *Hamlet* in funny voices, and how they laughed in the kitchen. She urged Maggie to walk back to Jesse's room with her, and after they had stood there for a moment, Franny started crying and went to the kitchen sink for a paper towel.

Maggie sat on Jesse's bed. A wave of sadness came over her, and unconsciously she uncovered Jesse's pillow, slipping her hands underneath. Feeling something, she lifted the pillow and found eight or nine scraps of paper, perhaps a note that had been torn up, but not very carefully. She slipped the scraps into her pocket.

–8–

Dreadful Note of Preparation

Maggie hugged Franny goodbye, packed up her picnic basket, and drove off. She only went a couple of blocks before pulling over to examine her find. Spreading the pieces out on the seat, she completed the puzzle. It was typed in large Arial font.

"Well now, Jesse," she said aloud, "that's an interesting thing to keep." She slipped the pieces back into her pocket.

On the drive home, Maggie took a detour, turning north down to the road that ran along the Ohio River. She needed time to think, and the river always quieted her mind. She loved the groves of eastern cottonwoods and willow trees that shaded the riverbank in summer. This stretch of River Road seemed to put her in touch with a longing that at once intrigued and frustrated her, as if she knew something she wasn't aware she knew. Stopping at the side of the road, she looked up to the bluff that rose above the riverbank.

In one of the tallest of the cottonwoods, a family of eagles had nested. Light filtered through the trees, and the sun-dappled grass seemed to move as if fairies were dancing there.

Maggie looked upriver.

Near the shore at some distance she saw the figure of Henry Bibb, a slave born in Shelby County, Kentucky, who ran away first at the age of ten and then at least six more times before he succeeded in reaching Detroit in 1841. As Maggie saw him, he was squatting near a burnt- out campfire, arranging his few belongings in a knapsack. She knew it to be the night he was escaping from the Gatewood plantation; he would soon be fording the Ohio just above Hagan's Crossing. Sadness swept through her because she knew he would be recaptured and sold downriver before his eventual escape to freedom.

Within seconds the image and feelings had passed.

Two sightings in one day. I feel like someone's reaching out to me, Maggie thought. This had happened to her so many times before that she had come to trust this second sight as a mysterious gift.

Suddenly she realized she wasn't alone.

"Well, Maggie O'Malley. It's a surprise to see you here."

The speaker was Marshall Hardy, a retired pharmacist and a birder who was also a local historian of sorts. He was wearing a black denim jacket with silver buttons and black jeans. The matching silver belt buckle gleamed in the sunshine . . . as did the short scythe he carried.

He took a swipe at the tall grass on his right.

Maggie knew that Marshall had a house nearby on the Old Post Road. His attachment to the land and the river showed in his sun-creased skin and rough hands. A permanent squint from years of watching light reflect off the rippling water added to his down-turned mouth, resulting in a scowl that dominated his face. His voice seemed to scowl as well.

"Hello, Marshall. I'm just here for a minute to check on the eagles. Are they in the nest?"

"The female is. I saw the male swoop out over the river about 15 minutes ago. You know that the cottonwood where they're nesting is probably 200 years old." This was a defining trait of Marshall's. He was always launching into mini-lectures, answering questions no one had asked. *A mansplainer*, she thought. *He can't help himself.*

"That tree shows up in an 1860 photograph of the plantation that once stood here. The tree was fairly tall even then. And about 500 yards upriver was the original ferry landing."

"Yes, I know. That's how the town got its name, Hagan's Crossing."

Marshall grimaced.

"Uh-huh. But the family who built the plantation that stood here didn't much like that. The whole town shouldn't have been named after that 'mick' ferryman." He looked out over the land leading to the river with a grim smile of satisfaction. "They were a higher-class family than all those Irish who came here."

Maggie laughed. "Remember you're talking to an O'Malley, Marshall."

He twisted his mouth into a forced smile. She steered the conversation in another direction.

"I know there was a plantation here before the Civil War."

Marshall's eyes lit up. "It was a fine, elegant place," he said. "They grew tobacco and kept a farm, and being on the river, it was like a summer place for the extended Speed clan—folks up near Louisville and down in Bardstown—there was quite a large family."

His tone struck Maggie as a bit proprietary. You'd have thought it was his plantation. But then, she reminded herself, Marshall was an unusual man. He had lived up here near the river all his life, and he had never married. Maggie remembered he'd had a younger sister, Mary Ann, from whom he'd become estranged. She had moved away and had died in an accident some years before.

Now, though, the name "Speed" had caught her attention, and she asked if descendants of the family still owned the land.

"No," Marshall said with no elaboration.

Maggie looked quizzically at him.

"Do you know a lot about the Speed family, Marshall?"

"A fair amount," he replied. "Why?"

"I dunno, I guess because you mentioned them."

"They were important people," he said gruffly.

Marshall had inched closer toward Maggie as he talked, and she made a pretext of backing up to peer across the river with her binoculars. As he turned and walked abruptly away, Maggie noticed how very thin Marshall was.

A strange bird, she thought.

–9–

The Mind's Construction in the Face

After seeing Maggie out, Franny returned to the kitchen to find her Yorkshire terrier, Cecil, planted in front of his bowl. He whined plaintively.

"I know, I know. It's time I did something nice for you, buddy."

Franny took a bag of cooked chicken and two eggs from the refrigerator. She chopped a chicken thigh into small pieces and sprayed a little cooking oil into a small skillet. Cecil sat perfectly still, waiting, but watching her closely. She scrambled the eggs in a bowl, added the chicken, and tossed the mixture into the heated skillet. Cecil began a little prance to show his excitement. He loved chicken omelets more than anything.

"You're a good boy, aren't you? Yes, you are. And I went out on the porch for so long and left you all by yourself, and you thought maybe you would starve to death." She kept talking just long enough for the food to cool and then put it in a clean bowl.

"That's for my special baby," she said, scratching the top of Cecil's head before settling into a chair while he ate.

Franny looked pensively around the large kitchen, its four smaller windows facing the back porch and the garden beyond, its larger window on the right wall facing the wraparound porch. To the far left was the back door, with an antique transom of stained glass depicting clusters of deep purple grapes on a trellised vine. A back stairway led up to the second floor. Dark green wainscoting complemented the light sage walls and open shelves. A tin ceiling, crown molding, and woodwork, all in white, made the room seem naturally light and airy.

This was one of Franny's favorite rooms. The large oak table showed the use of three generations, and she appreciated every nick and scrape. Her grandmother had taught her to make biscuits on this table. Sometimes she would pass her hand over the spot at the end, closest to the corner pantry, where her mother always kneaded bread, and she would think how odd it was to miss her mother after 50 years.

Enjoying the breeze from the windows she kept open, she closed her eyes and thought about the Sunday dinners the three women had cooked together in this kitchen, at this table. She could almost hear the voices and laughter—and her grandmother pounding the chicken with a mallet—no, wait. She opened her eyes and realized that was the sound of someone knocking at the front door.

"Hold on, now," she called out on the way down the hall. She could see through the sidelight the figure of a man whose hand was raised to knock again as she swung the door open.

"May I help you?" she asked in greeting.

"I'm sorry, ma'am, to disturb you. I'm looking for a young man I believe lives here, Mr. Jesse Gilemorane."

The man was tall with the effect of being scrawny, in his early 50s, with graying dark brown hair and a trimmed beard. He wore a beige linen suit with a pale blue shirt and navy bow tie. His brown shoes looked newly polished. Still, Miss Babcock looked at his narrow eyes and creased smile and decided she did not trust him. She didn't invite him in but came out onto the porch and gestured for him to sit in a white wicker chair. Disappointment flickered across his face.

"Is Mr. Gilemorane at home?" he asked.

"No, I'm afraid not," she said.

"Do you know when he'll return?"

"No, I can't say I do."

The visitor felt her resistance and took a deep breath.

"He contacted me. My name is Avery G. Prendergast. I'm a historian of sorts, a broker, an expert in historical documents and ephemera."

"Oh really?" she replied.

"Yes, ma'am. Mr. Gilemorane said that he had knowledge of a large number of documents, some of which might be valuable. As I'm attending a conference at McLaughlin College, I thought I would stop. I tried to call, but the number I had was disconnected."

Franny continued to eye the man suspiciously, wondering why Jesse would be looking for a way to sell her documents. To her knowledge, Jesse didn't even have a cell phone. She noticed that the afternoon sun on the man's wrinkled forehead was blossoming into beads of sweat, which he blotted with a handkerchief.

"I'm wondering, ma'am, if you would perhaps let me take a look at the materials Mr. Gilemorane referenced. Are they accessible?"

"No, I think not. Not to be rude, but I do not know you or

know why Mr. Gilemorane would have contacted you. To my knowledge, he doesn't own any such documents."

Prendergast looked at her steely blue eyes and thought what a good liar she was. Of course, Jesse had told him about the elderly woman and the source of the trunks, but she was gonna play dumb. He hoped this deal was going to be worth the trouble. He smiled at her and softened his manner.

"Ma'am, I certainly understand why you would be cautious in talking with a stranger about this. You might be worried that the historical nature of these papers could make them attractive to dishonest people. The truth is, Jesse is my nephew, my sister Gina's boy, and he said he wanted advice about how to get a valid appraisal of the collection for your benefit. Do you happen to know what's in the papers?"

He was afraid she was going to deny their existence altogether, but she hesitated just long enough to make the lie implausible.

"No, I don't. Where are you from, Mr. Prendergast?"

"The Cleveland area."

"And you said you were traveling—why?"

"For business," he said. "I've been attending a humanities conference in town, and now I'm on my way to view a collection of Mary Todd Lincoln ephemera in Lexington. I'm sure you know she grew up there in a house on Main Street. Of course, I should go on to Hodgenville; I'm a Lincoln fan but have never seen the birthplace."

Miss Babcock maintained the pretense that she knew nothing of the documents, and Prendergast continued to act as if he knew they were at hand. He made one more try.

"You can trust me, ma'am," he said.

"Well, sir, I doubt that. I don't know why you didn't introduce yourself as Jesse's uncle at the outset. I hope you'll pardon me for ending your visit."

She stood up, turning her back to him, and went into the house.

Franny watched through the corner of the window until he pulled away. He was driving a white Ford Fiesta, probably a rental car; it seemed too shiny to be his own car driven all the way from Cleveland. She looked at her watch—3:30 p.m.—and debated taking her afternoon nap. Perhaps she should call Chief Callahan and tell him a man was looking for Jesse. Maybe later. She decided to lie down; she was tired to the bone.

"But first I have to arrange to have those trunks taken over to Maggie's house," she said aloud.

She made the phone call to her handyman, and Robert agreed that he and his boy would come over right after supper. Franny phoned Maggie: there was no answer, so she left a message to expect the delivery around 8:00, adding that she wanted Maggie to keep the documents.

Franny's bedroom was her second-favorite room in the house. The wallpaper, inspired by a William Morris acanthus design, gave the room a Pre-Raphaelite air.

For years Franny had used a larger bedroom on the second floor, but in her mid-70s she'd decided to move to this first floor middle room, away from the noise of the street and the back door. This meant she didn't hear Jesse coming or going, a fact she regretted just now—but she simply had to lie down. Stretching out on top of the cotton sateen duvet, she pulled a lap quilt made by her mother up over her legs and closed her eyes.

Within minutes, she had slipped into a dream—a strange one, in which a turtle wearing a Cleveland cap was riding down the street in a red teacup and she was expected to catch him to make turtle soup. Following that, she dreamt that her great-grandfather had come back from a long trip and wanted something that was in the trunks. He said he couldn't come inside because there were clocks in the house. He stood out on the front sidewalk and extended his arm all the way into the house through the front window, feeling around the library until he lifted a paper from the middle of the pile. It started glowing when he touched it, so he knew it was what he had come for. His arm retracted just as magically, and as he folded the paper and put it inside his coat pocket, the bright glow diminished.

Franny woke with a start. The feeling of awe she had felt in the dream—seeing her great- grandfather magically reach into the house and lift out the luminous paper—lingered. *He couldn't come in because there were clocks in the house*, she thought. *That's odd.* She lay still for a few minutes, thinking of the dream and of all the members of her family who had lived and died in this house.

She thought she heard a noise in the kitchen. Slowly, she got up and eased her way down the hall to the back of the house. No one. The clock said 6:07.

Going into her sitting room, she settled in her recliner and switched on the news, drowning out the footsteps on the back porch.

–10–

A Local Habitation and a Name

While Franny napped, Maggie dug further into the Babcock genealogy. She discovered that Franny's great-great-grandfather, Isaac S. Caldwell Sr., had practiced law in Louisville from 1832 to 1877, joined by his son Isaac Jr. in 1852. They were prominent citizens in those crucial decades when the city at the Falls of the Ohio became a gateway to the west and south. They counted among their friends the men who instituted the Louisville Lyceum, the Kentucky Historical Society, and the city's first medical college.

According to the 1870 census, Isaac Jr. lived with his father, his mother Frances, and a brother and sister, Catherine and George, in a fashionable part of Louisville. They had an Irish- born maid, Brigid, and a Black cook, Ada.

In 1881, with the admission of Isaac S. Caldwell III to the bar, the family removed themselves to the countryside of Hagan's Crossing and built a suitable Queen Anne home. Trips back and forth to Louisville in their fine carriage afforded them the opportunity to contemplate their greatness.

Maggie found that among Isaac Caldwell Sr.'s clients were Judge John Speed of Farmington, a large plantation in Kentucky; John Jeremiah Jacob, a builder and financier who became the first millionaire in Louisville; his partner, Thomas Prather; and George Keats, brother of the poet John Keats. George Keats had invested in lumber and flour mills, speculated in real estate, and built a Greek Revival mansion on Walnut Street. She did some reading from the prominent men's biographies.

She remembered that Jimmy had asked her to look up the Gilemorane genealogy, and she spent about an hour searching. Since the most recently released census was from 1940, Jesse himself was too young to turn up in those records. Maggie couldn't find the surname in any Kentucky or Ohio birth records either.

The grandfather clock struck 8:00, and Maggie remembered she hadn't called Mary Lou to confirm their meeting the next day at Mary Lou's café. It was primarily on Mary Lou's behalf that Maggie had spent a week in May at the National Archives in Washington, DC, looking at records from the Freedmen's Bureau. She had been researching her friend's ancestry in addition to working on some smaller projects.

She and Mary Lou had gone to high school together and were partners on the debate team for a year, but Maggie had never been to Mary Lou's house growing up. Like many small towns in Kentucky, Hagan's Crossing had desegregated its schools in the early '60s, long before the large cities did, but neighborhoods were not integrated when Maggie and Mary Lou were children. The Johnsons had been one of about 30 Black families living in a segregated part of Hagan's Crossing called Davis Creek. Mary Lou had lived with her parents, her three brothers, her grandmother and great-aunt, and two uncles in a three-story farmhouse there.

They agreed to meet at 10:00 the next morning. Then Robert and his son arrived with Franny's trunks. It took about 20 minutes to get them into the house and arranged in the spare room. Before going to bed, Maggie called Franny to say that the trunks were safely stored.

"This is a good omen, Maggie." Franny explained that she was especially grateful to have the papers out of her house because a pushy man had visited her that afternoon, insisting that Jesse had invited him to see her valuable documents.

"He even claimed to be Jesse's uncle—said Jesse was his sister Gina's boy. I knew that was a lie because Jesse once mentioned his mother's name, and it was something else—two names, like Ann Marie. But I didn't say so. Oh Maggie, thank God the papers are gone," she said. "I trust that if you find anything of real value, you'll let me know. I'd like you to keep the papers for your research. Consider them yours."

"Okay, Franny. Thank you."

After hanging up, Maggie sat for a moment thinking about the man she had met at the reception, the one who traded in documents. *What did he say his name was? Could he have been the one who visited Franny? Was he really someone Jesse knew?*

-11-

What's Past is Prologue

The Cup 'n Saucer was a small café tucked between a photographer's studio and an insurance broker on Poplar Street in downtown Hagan's Crossing. The interior reflected the decades it had been a fixture in the business district: a third of the tables were metal, enameled in red and white, from the 1940s; another third were yellow and white Formica and chrome from the '50s; the remainder were a mixture of real and faux wood designs, with mismatched chairs. The varied styles appealed to Maggie's sense of history.

Maggie was early, and taking a seat in front of the window, she wondered at the origins of the menagerie of napkin holders and salt and pepper shakers dotting the tables. The theme was American farmhouse. Shaped like owls, chickens, kittens, and sheep, the items were all secondhand, rescued from flea markets. Maggie thought about all the housewives who had filled their kitchens with cows that poured milk, pigs that hoarded cookies, and roosters that told time. *Mary Lou has made this place feel so homey*, Maggie thought. *It's like stepping back into the past.*

The entry bell on the front door tinkled and Maggie looked up to see Mary Lou, dressed in jeans and a colorful kente cloth shirt in orange, green, and gold. Maggie stood up and the two women hugged.

"Girl, I've missed you," Mary Lou said. "I'm so glad we could do this."

"Me too," Maggie said.

Just then, a car slowly driving by caught her eye—a maroon Chevy with a driver who seemed to be scanning the street as if looking for an address. She wondered if he might be the man whose appearances in the neighborhood had alarmed Miss Babcock.

Mary Lou noticed her distraction. "What's so interesting out there?"

Maggie explained Franny's anxiety over the man in the maroon car who seemed to be watching her house.

"That's spooky," Mary Lou said. "Has she called the police?"

"No," Maggie said, "but I wish she would. Maybe I'll tell Jimmy myself."

"I wouldn't want to be living alone in that big old house," Mary Lou said. "She's a sitting duck, especially with so many antiques. Now, I want you to tell me everything about the murder at the play Thursday, but let's order first. You want the usual? The full breakfast?"

Maggie agreed, and Mary Lou asked the waitress for two full breakfasts, adding a warning to Denice not to be skimpy on the pancakes.

"Okay, now—tell me. I heard that the murder happened onstage! Were you close? Was there blood? Did you know it had happened right away? Tell me!"

Maggie began narrating the events—with appropriate suspense—but when she came to the images of the "poisoning" and the twitching body and Anna's screaming, Mary Lou said, "Oh, stop. No. How horrible."

"It was horrible. Everything turned to chaos in a few seconds," Maggie said.

"So, was it a real poisoning?"

"They don't have the toxicology report yet—probably not until Monday. It looks like a poisoning, definitely suspicious."

Maggie described her visit to Anna and her lunch with Franny, ending with an admission that she had agreed to take the trunks of papers.

"Uh-oh, Mags, are you getting yourself involved in this business? I know how you are. Do you really think it's safe to have any part of it? That kid Jesse is still missing, isn't he?"

"I'll be careful," Maggie said. "Promise."

"I do worry about you, Mags. You need some protection. Maybe you should get a small 9 mm like mine," Mary Lou said.

"You own a gun? I never knew that!"

"I bought myself a little Glock 43 to carry when I have to take receipts to the bank drop box late at night. I got a concealed carry permit, and I practice at the range once a month. Of course, I hope I never have to use it," Mary Lou said.

"Well, I understand your reasoning, but I would end up shooting myself. I'm safer without a gun," Maggie said.

Mary Lou made an exaggerated frown, and they fell silent.

Maggie changed the subject to Mary Lou's genealogy, taking some notes out of her purse.

She handed a couple of pages to Mary Lou.

"You are going to be so excited when I show you what I

found! And the best part came from Franny's papers. It was a total coincidence that the first things I saw were records from Farmington. But—wait, I'm getting ahead of myself. First we work backward."

Maggie's eyes were sparkling with excitement.

"I started with your mother, born in 1910. She shows up in the 1920 census, where her name is recorded as Alese. Wasn't it Alice?"

Mary Lou nodded.

"Her mother is listed as Bella Goode and her father as Charles Goode. Going back a generation, I found your grandmother as Isabella in the 1880 census, when she was three years old. In the 1900 census, she is listed as Izzy, aged 20—but census data was often given by neighbors, so ages can be way off.

"From the Freedmen's Bureau records, I found that your great-grandmother was Cassie Jackson, born at Farmington in about 1843. She married an older man named Joseph Clark, although the marriage was not recognized legally. It was before the war. She was the daughter of a woman named Athena, who was probably born in the 1820s."

"Athena—that's new," Mary Lou said. "Very classical. I guess it was chosen by a white slaveholder. And I never knew Cassie's husband's name was Joseph. Of course, I knew Grandma Izzy."

"Did you know Cassie was enslaved at Farmington?"

Maggie pulled out copies she had made of the Speed papers but didn't hand them across the table.

Mary Lou sat for a minute, an elbow propped in front of her. Leaning her cheek on her closed fist, she smiled crookedly.

"Yeah, she—well, there were family stories. Don't know exactly what's true and what isn't."

Maggie could feel Mary Lou's sadness as she began talking about Cassie. According to family lore, Mary Lou explained, Cassie's mother had been "a favorite" of one of the Speed gentlemen—maybe a cousin—and Cassie was born so light-complected that they raised her in the big house and treated her like a doll. When the second plantation house was built up on the river, Cassie, not yet five years old, was given to one of John Speed's sons—just taken from her mother at Farmington. Athena's violent reaction caused them to sell her off at the slave market.

"I don't know if that's true, but that's the story," Mary Lou concluded.

Maggie handed Mary Lou copies of the Speed letters.

"It is true. Here's the letter about selling Athena down the river. They wanted her out of the state altogether. It's horrible," Maggie said. "And it explains why I didn't find Athena in any Kentucky records during Reconstruction. I wonder if we can trace her—if there are any more documents about the transaction in the lawyers' papers. The documents are all jumbled up in the trunks, so I'll have to see what turns up."

Mary Lou silently read the letter.

"Do you think Athena was brought from Africa?" Mary Lou asked.

"No, but maybe one of her parents was. The importation of slaves stopped in 1808," Maggie said. "But the Spanish had brought slaves to South Carolina as early as the 1520s, and a half million Africans had been enslaved and brought to the Americas before what's generally considered the beginning of slavery in the colonies, at Jamestown in 1619. The business of enslavement was much bigger than most people realize."

Mary Lou shook her head and looked down at the table. "Sometimes I think of Cassie and how she must have felt, being treated like a plaything—probably pampered as a toddler and little girl—until she realized she was a piece of property. It's interesting that now the Farmington people call the slaves 'enslaved Africans.' Supposed to make us feel better, I guess."

"I think it's in the interest of historical accuracy," Maggie replied. "Instead of owners, we should say enslavers. And runaway slaves should be freedom seekers. There are even people who argue that the word 'plantation' evokes magnolia blossoms and romance; they'd prefer the sites be called 'enslavement camps.'"

Maggie asked what Mary Lou knew about the second plantation, Endymion, and its owners.

"Not much. My grandma called it 'Indiaman.' When I was little, I thought she was saying 'Indian-man.'"

It seemed to Maggie, as Mary Lou talked, that the shadow of her great-grandmother drew near—not that she was visible, but Maggie could feel the lamentation of generations of Black women in Mary Lou's voice: first the agony of Athena at having her child ripped away from her and the bitter fate of being sold downriver, then the trials of Cassie, who had been raised at Endymion and had never seen her mother again. At 17, Cassie had been paired with a man decades older than she. Maybe she had loved her husband, but her choice wouldn't have mattered.

Mary Lou said her grandmother had told her that when the war ended, Cassie and her husband stayed with the Speed family as servants, not seeing any sense in leaving a place that was safe. Cassie had several children who died. Only one baby, Mary Lou's grandmother Isabella—who had been born late to them—survived.

According to the family story, Cassie's husband was murdered when Isabella was only one or two years old. When the Speeds sold the property, Cassie moved to the Black section of town, where she raised Isabella by washing for white families in Hagan's Crossing.

"My mama said that her mama used to tell the stories from way back as if they had just happened last year—and had happened to her, not to her mother—they were so real to her. Mama used to joke with us that we ought to all show up at Farmington one day and tell the folks there that we had come for our inheritance. She would always add, "Cause all y'all are Speeds, you know."' Mary Lou laughed at the thought of it.

"If the family story is true, you *are* Speeds!" Maggie said.

"Maybe," Mary Lou answered. Then, going into her best Hattie McDaniel impression, "But that don't mean massa gonna share none o' the hidden treasure wid us."

The waitress appeared with two trays bearing Denice's culinary masterpieces. Tall, fluffy stacks of pancakes with butter melting over the sides. Eggs, bacon, grits, fried potatoes, coffee, and orange juice. The food covered every inch of the table. Mary Lou started by drizzling pure maple syrup over her pancakes.

"Mmmm, mmmm, these are delicious," she said, "even if I say so myself."

Maggie started in on the pancakes as well.

"You were saying something about a treasure. Was there really a treasure?" Maggie asked.

"Oh, it's just a lot of fool stories. For one thing, Cassie wasn't the only Black woman who carried a white man's child; Mama said the white man might have been one of the sons or cousins of the family or even guests who would spend the night. It was common to have a bed for travelers needing a place, and Farmington had one. I reckon some men might have considered having sex with an enslaved woman one of the amenities."

"Oh, what a nightmare. I can't begin to fathom the kind of cruelty it took to own slaves," Maggie said.

"And John Speed was said to be against slavery. Mm, mm, mm," Mary Lou said, shaking her head.

They were both silent for a moment, thinking soberly. Then Maggie said, "Wait, go back to the treasure—what was the treasure?"

"It's just stories. There was supposed to be a wooden chest. One story is that it was taken to Endymion and buried on the property. Mama said the idea that there was gold and silver and jewels was just crazy."

Maggie thought for a minute. "It could have been documents related to the plantation," she said. "John Speed died in 1840. It might be that right after his death, some of his papers were taken out of the house. I wonder how many Speed descendants still live in this area. The family tree is hard to keep straight. I've seen published versions without dates for births, deaths, and marriages, and there was marriage across generations—like one grandson of Judge Speed marrying the younger sister of his uncle's wife. I've read that when the Speeds had a Fourth of July picnic in 1881, 107 family members were present!"

"Dang," Mary Lou said. "And those were just the white folks!"

Maggie laughed. Then she proposed they ride out to the site of the plantation, by the river, stopping in to visit Marshall Hardy, who lived nearby.

"I think Marshall knows something about that place," Maggie said.

Mary Lou agreed.

As they were about to leave, however, a couple of patrons stopped on their way out to compliment Mary Lou on the success of the Cup 'n Saucer, and they got into a conversation. Maggie sat back down to be polite. Glancing out the window, she saw what she thought was the tail end of the maroon Chevy.

"I'm gonna find out who that guy is," she said aloud.

Calling the police station, Maggie was put through to Jimmy's voice mail, where she left a message explaining Franny Babcock's anxiety about the maroon car and her own observation of the driver's unusual behavior.

Maggie, Maggie, there you go—it was her mother's voice in her head—*minding other people's business again.*

"That's right, Mama," she said out loud.

~12~

The Evil That Men Do

1800, West Africa

Akosua worked under the shade of the palm tree next to the family hut. At nearly ten years old, she would have gone into the yam fields with her mother this day except that her older brother had been sick in the night with stomach pain, and her mother had left Akosua to tend to him. Their father had gone hunting during the last new moon, and the young girl looked expectantly for his return every morning. Fifteen-year-old Addae was now sleeping, having drunk the acacia tea his mother had forced on him.

Akosua had been busying herself with sorting yams by size, preparing them for curing in a large pile of dry grass and wood ash under jute bags. Newly gathered yams needed to be properly cured before being stacked in the vertical yam barns. She did not mind this work because it gave her time to recount out loud the stories of the tricky spider, Anansi, imitating the silly voices her father used when he entertained the family with nightly folk tales.

The sun was rising high above the village, and Akosua wondered if Addae was feeling better. Putting the yams aside, she went into the darkened hut. Addae was sitting up, drinking water from a gourd. He assured Akosua he was perfectly well and urged her to go with him to the yam fields. He stood up and, leaving the hut, strode quickly away toward the edge of the village.

Although she objected, Akosua could only follow him, and she had to run because his stride was so long. A quarter mile from the village, a tributary of the river crossed their path. Parallel to the stream was a sacred grove of trees, an area children did not enter. Between the grove and the water, thick shrubbery formed a living fence.

On the opposite shore, partly draped over the shrubbery, an amazing display of colors— scarves of vivid red, yellow, and blue—caught their attention. Strings of colored beads also lay in piles on the bank, and metal shards hung on lengths of string being blown erratically by the wind. Akosua stood in amazement at the ringing sounds, thinking the musical shards flittered around one another like shiny singing birds.

Addae took her by the arm, pulling her across the stream and up the bank to reach the enticing trinkets. He looked around and, seeing no one, squatted to pick up the necklaces and shake them to catch the sunlight. Akosua lifted a red scarf from the grass, playfully wrapping it around her head.

Without warning, four men jumped out of the shrubbery, two grabbing Akosua and two grabbing her brother. In a matter of minutes the helpless children's hands were bound with stout ropes and their mouths were gagged. They lay squirming on the ground.

Akosua did not recognize the attackers. *They are not Akan or Ashanti*, she thought.

One of the men lifted Akosua to a standing position and pushed her roughly, causing Addae to try to scramble to his feet, but with his hands bound, he could get no purchase. Another man yanked him up, growling angrily. Three of the men kept the children penned in while the fourth gathered up the scarves and beads and took down the singing metal birds.

Then they set out on a branching path heading to the southwest, away from the village, away from the yam fields, and into the forest. One man led while another pushed Akosua ahead of him, followed by Addae, with the last two men bringing up the rear, occasionally prodding the boy with one of the metal sticks.

Akosua's bewilderment had turned to fear and then to anger. She and Addae had been tricked by the men just as Anansi had tricked the leopard and the snake and had so captured them. She wondered if these men were spirits like the ones who had made Anansi's head fall off, or if they had come from the sky god. She wanted to ask Addae what he thought, but talking was impossible.

For three more days the men marched the two children south, giving them water only once and tying their feet tightly at night to prevent escape. At least at night Akosua could curl up in the arc of Addae's body and feel his strong heart beating. When Akosua struggled to keep up the pace, one of their captors grew impatient and, lifting her under the crook of her arm, dragged her though the thick foliage. Her bare legs were cut and bleeding from the thorns of the gàblìgá. On the third day, she was so slow that the leader forced Addae to carry her on his back through the heat of the day. The men seemed increasingly anxious to keep moving quickly and more than once used a spear to poke Addae and Akosua in the back.

At night on the third day, they came to a clearing and a beach, although the darkness concealed the expanse of ocean. There were dozens of strange men, as pale as the moon, with what looked like jute strings hanging from their heads. The hair that ought to have been on their heads was on their faces. They were covered, too, in cloth that hid their arms and legs, and they carried long metal sticks which they pointed menacingly.

Also in the clearing were hundreds of Africans from tribes Akosua did not recognize. The tribesmen were tied around their waists with ropes, binding them in groups of about 20. In the light of flickering campfires, she saw faces carved in anger and sorrow, men and women slumped in dejection and grief. Akosua had not cried through all these days because she had told herself it was only a story, only a seeming tragedy created by the Trickster Spider, and her father was sure to appear around the next bend in the road to rescue them. Now, however, she saw and felt the truth. She and Addae were not going to be found, were not going to return to their parents ever again.

In the harbor, a tall wooden ship with wide white sails rose above the scene, its gangplank lowered to the shore. Despite the darkness, groups of Africans were being forced onto the ship and down into its hold. Torches only partially revealed what was happening; the rest was conveyed by sound—the whips cracking against human flesh, the crying out and moaning, the clanking of iron chains and shackles being snapped into place.

The pale men sounded like wild, barking dogs. Some laughed as they stripped the remaining clothing off the new arrivals. Akosua was pulled away from Addae and shoved into a group of women who were then pushed down a wooden plank and forced to lie side by side on the wet wooden floor.

Akosua saw herself as one of the yams lined up for curing. Now she began to cry.

For the next 64 days the ship weathered the storms of the Atlantic. The 402 captured Africans suffered from stifling heat, dysentery, and fever. Feces and vomit soon covered the floor. Conditions were so wretched that by three weeks into the voyage contagion was rampant, and the ship's captain had thrown 32 persons overboard, most—but not all—dead. The ship's insurance would not cover a loss by death from illness, but the expense of an enslaved person "lost overboard" could be recouped.

Akosua could not see Addae from where she was chained, and on the mornings she was taken up onto the deck, she could only glimpse the back of his head for a moment from the plank. At least he was still alive. *Still alive* was one of the few thoughts she seemed able to form in her mind.

Most of the time she ceased to think and became a series of sensations—endless rocking, rising, and falling with the ocean as if she were part of the waves that bore her farther and farther away from herself. *Akosua.* She would whisper her name as if to remember it. It meant she was born on a Sunday. She would say "Addae, Addae, Addae," wishing he could hear her. His name meant "morning sun." She began a ritual for each time she was led up onto the deck: looking at his head, she would chant his name, then raising her face to the sky, she would say, "Still alive." What more could she do to hang on to life?

The ship docked in a foreign place, the largest village Akosua could imagine, with hundreds of the pale people in control of everything. Taken from the ship, the Africans were pushed into cages in an open-air marketplace. Two or three at a time, they were taken from the cages and chained to stakes, where the pale men doused them with buckets of water.

Some who had lain in their own waste for weeks were caked with a crust that took soapy water and a hard brushing to remove. Scabbed-over sores were reopened, and the black bodies writhed in pain. Those healthy enough to be sold right away were rubbed in hog grease to make their skin shiny. Then they were taken to the auction block.

Akosua watched as Addae, naked and miserable, endured this process. She called out his name as he was put on display, and when he turned toward her, she saw that the entire right side of his face had been deeply scarred, whether by burning or beating she could not tell. He looked down and away in shame. It was the last she saw of him, as he was purchased and led away. When her turn came to be led onto the block, she was paired with another girl about a foot taller and maybe three years older. Although she could not understand the auctioneer's speech, she knew what he intended to show as he cupped each of her budding breasts in turn with his right hand and lifted her chin before stroking her neck.

The two girls were bought together by a man who ran his hands over their bare skin and between their thighs before handing them cotton shifts to put on.

"Lord knows I can't take you home naked, though I doubt you'd know the difference," he said. Resting his palm on Akosua's chest, he said, "Your name is Susan Ford." Touching his own chest, he said, "I am Massa Ford. You belong to me. Say 'Susan Ford.'"

Touching her breast, she said, "Akosua," and he slapped her sharply upside the head.

"Su-san-Ford. Su-san-Ford." He continued until she

repeated the name, then turned his attention to the other girl, whom he named "Sally."

Shackled together, they were both loaded onto the bed of a farm wagon, along with sacks of flour and sugar the man had purchased. Before mounting the seat, he chained the larger girl's ankle to the bed of the wagon. "Jest in case you think of jumping out," he said with a hollow laugh. "I'd hate to have to drag you home, but I will if need be."

Akosua squeezed the hand of the other girl and shook with silent sobs, thinking of her mother.

Genealogy of Mary Lou Johnson

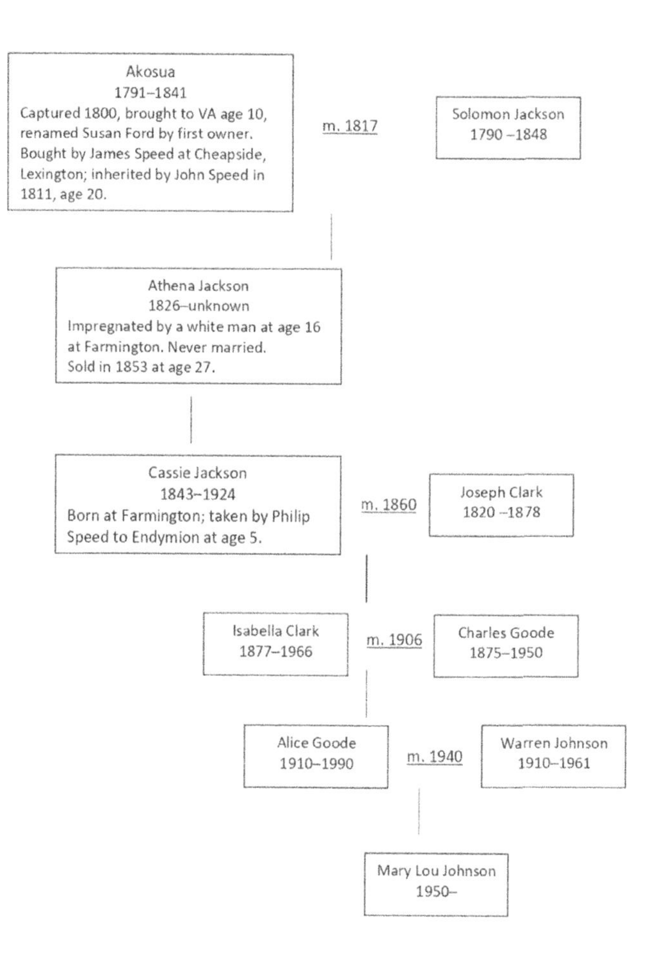

–13–

I Could a Tale Unfold

On their drive toward the river, Mary Lou talked to Maggie about her grandmother and added an intriguing detail about her great-grandmother. "Grandma said that Cassie was hell-bent on everybody going to school and learning to read and write. She was always buying secondhand books. Some folks laughed at her about that, but learning was always first in our family," she said.

Marshall Hardy's cabin was up a gravel road that led to a plateau, giving him a clear view of the river. It was a nicer place than Maggie had expected, a commercially built log cabin surrounded by poplars and dogwoods, with bird feeders hanging on every available branch. Marshall had done some landscaping too, with wildflowers that added to the rustic setting. Pulling up in front of the cabin, Maggie saw that the road made a circle around the house; Marshall had no neighbors on the Old Post Road. He was standing on the front porch that spanned the width of the cabin, having stood up from one of the wooden rocking chairs when he heard Maggie's car.

The day was heating up, and cicadas in the trees between Marshall's house and the river sang multiple choruses set to different tempos. Still, there was a breeze that Maggie hadn't felt in town; close to the river was always cooler. Marshall, as usual, was wearing black denim jeans and jacket.

"Ah, Maggie. Back again?"

"Hi, Marshall," Maggie said as they approached the porch. "You know Mary Lou Johnson, don't you? She owns the Cup 'n Saucer in town."

"Yes, I certainly do. Hi." He put out his hand to Mary Lou.

Looking at Maggie, Marshall said, "Say, have you heard any more about the kid who got killed during the Shakespeare play? After you left yesterday, I wished I had asked you about it. You were there, right? I wasn't."

Maggie recounted the bare bones, hoping to leave it at that, but Marshall asked several more questions about the two actors. Maggie felt he was pushing her to speculate on what the police were thinking. Finally she said, "That's all I know, Marshall. Really." He let go of the topic reluctantly.

"Well, then, what brings you out here on a Saturday morning?" he asked.

"We just had breakfast and got to talking about local history and thought we'd come out to ask you some questions. Mary Lou was telling me about that small plantation house that used to be around here. The one you were talking about yesterday."

Marshall gestured for the two women to be seated on the porch, and he returned to his rocker. The curve of its rattan seat testified to the hours Marshall had spent sitting there. At his side was a colander filled with green beans he had been snapping, and he picked it up to continue.

"Yes," he said, "a man named Rankin first had a small cabin over there closer to the creek, but then he started to build a

12-room house on the bluff and planted tobacco and hemp in the fields to the south. He got real sick, though, and he sold the property, house unfinished, to one of the Speed brothers. He'd cleared about 200 acres, but that wasn't nearly as big as Judge John Speed's plantation, Farmington."

"What happened then?"

"The Speed brother finished the house and moved here as a summer home, mostly; his father had died, and another member of the family had bought Farmington. He had a house down in Louisville too."

Marshall's demeanor was a curious mixture of reticence and pride, as if he had plenty of details to share—and wanted to be recognized as an expert—but was weighing his words carefully.

"You know a lot of the history of this place," Mary Lou said.

"Yep. I've lived 'round here all my life. My grandpa told me stories he was told by his father, who worked for the Speeds, stories about runaway slaves trying to hide on the property and cross the Ohio from here—and being dragged back and chained to a spike in the yard, like dogs. He said the house had some high-toned visitors too. Friends of the Speeds were brought up here to escape the heat."

"Mary Lou's great-grandmother was enslaved at this plantation from about 1846; she came from Farmington," Maggie said.

Marshall looked startled.

"Really?" he said to Mary Lou. "Are you sure about that?"

"Yes," she said. "My grandmother lived with us and told me stories about my family."

"Uh-huh," he said.

"About the Speeds," she said.

Marshall looked at Mary Lou as if he expected her to explain further. She only smiled.

Marshall seemed a little irritated, as though Mary Lou and Maggie were trespassing on his piece of history. He didn't like being surprised.

Mary Lou continued, mentioning her great-grandfather who had been killed.

"I was hoping you might know about that story, Marshall," Maggie said. He shook his head no.

Mary Lou recounted the details of Cassie and Joseph living as servants of the Speeds after emancipation, including the rumors of a treasure supposedly transferred from Farmington to what her grandma called "Indiaman."

Marshall burst out laughing at the name, and Mary Lou stopped abruptly. With a patronizing tone, Marshall explained that the name of the plantation was Endymion, after a poem by John Keats.

"I know that," Mary Lou said quietly.

"No offense, Mary Lou, but I 'spect your family wasn't much on literary references," he said, "or poetry readings."

Both women looked at him in disbelief, taken aback by his continuing to relish the joke he thought he had made.

"Well, at the time," Mary Lou said, "they were at a disadvantage—being enslaved and all."

"Oh, now, don't get all het up," he interjected, but Maggie interrupted.

"Do you know the exact location of the house, Marshall?"

"Right here where we're sitting—on this plateau. It was razed during World War I."

"Oh my," Mary Lou said. She stood up, walked down the

steps, and approached the river to look toward the slow-moving water.

Even Marshall seemed to sense this was an emotional moment for Mary Lou, and he silently returned to snapping his beans. Maggie listened to the songs of the cicadas, realizing they were the same sounds Mary Lou's great-grandmother had listened to on this spot over 100 years before.

What was the line from Keats's "Ode to a Nightingale"? "Perhaps the self-same song that found a path through the sad heart of Ruth, when, sick for home, she stood in tears amid the alien corn . . ." Maggie had meditated on the starvation and hardship of her Irish ancestors during the Great Famine, but she knew it couldn't compare to the burden history had laid on Mary Lou.

After a few minutes, Mary Lou returned to the porch, her eyes moist. The three of them sat another full minute in silence.

"Just one more thing, Marshall," Maggie said at last. "Franny Babcock said she had some large trunks of legal papers dating back to the 1830s because her people were lawyers—and some of those might be Speed papers. She said she told you and some other folks about them. What do you know about the family that might shed light on those papers?"

Marshall stiffened. "Franny must be mistaken. She never told me about any trunks of papers. She's getting kinda forgetful, you know—and confused."

"You didn't know that she'd hired a young man to go through them for her?"

"Nope. I never heard a word about it," he said. Marshall had finished snapping the beans and stood up, which Maggie and Mary Lou took as a sign that they should go.

Back in the car, Mary Lou vented her feelings about Marshall's disdain for her family, suggesting that he would probably welcome back Jim Crow if he could. Maggie agreed that he had been condescending and especially abrupt.

"Living up there alone as he does, I think he forgets how to talk to people," Maggie said. "I don't think there's any malice in him."

After dropping off Mary Lou at the café, Maggie gave a lot of thought to Marshall Hardy's story. Overall, he had seemed petulant. Was he lying about not knowing the papers existed? Maggie decided to dig into those trunks and get a look at property records as well.

-14-

I Go, and It is Done

Early Sunday evening found Marshall Hardy walking down to the riverbank to watch the Ohio glide past him in the fading light. Pieces of driftwood, like so many little Loch Ness Monsters, would bob up, disappear, and bob up again several yards downriver. He followed them with his gaze, trying to predict when each one might surface again. He liked to imagine the whole 981 miles of the river as it snaked its way to the Mississippi.

In his mind's eye, he watched the Native Americans skim past in their light canoes, the paddlewheels churn through the black water, brightly lit and filled with revelers whose laughter was carried on the breeze with strains of a piano and banjo playing "Turkey in the Straw."

This river was his; this land was his. He deserved to get his full inheritance!

In the failing light, his eyes tracked a tow boat and three barges, loaded with coal, down the river, probably from West Virginia. As calm as the evening was, Marshall felt jittery. He kept replaying yesterday's conversation with Maggie and Mary Lou.

On the other side of town, parked in a shady section of Willow Lane, the man removed his Cleveland cap. Turning it over and over, lightly rubbing the inside and inspecting the underside of the bill, he ran his fingers over the embroidery. The cap had probably never been washed. Mark wouldn't have taken it off long enough to have it washed, and he certainly wouldn't have wanted anyone to reshape it; the hat had fit his head precisely. *He must have owned four dozen hats*, the man thought, *but the only one he wanted to wear was this one.* At this thought, the man felt his throat thicken with emotion. *No, none of that, now*, he thought. *Don't get sidetracked. You've got to stay focused. You know what has to be done.*

Eight blocks away, at Maggie's house, she had just finished a shower and pulled on some light shorts and a sleep shirt. She had been searching through Franny's papers all afternoon and had come across a letter from George Keats to his attorney. It fascinated her that the brother and sister-in-law of the famous English Romantic poet had settled in Louisville. Since that line from Keats had popped into her mind yesterday, she took this discovery as a sign that she ought to read some more of his poetry.

Without delay, Finn and Fiona both made an appearance, Finn being the first to climb onto her lap to sit on the opened book. Maggie, not deterred by this, pulled the book out and propped it on top of Finn while Fiona curled up next to her to nap.

Several miles away, in the woods by the river, Jesse was feeling more anxiety than ever. Three days of hiding hadn't made him feel safer. He knew what he had seen and what it meant. Going over the events again and again, he kept thinking he would find a solution, but he felt trapped. Leaving town without finishing what he had started wasn't an option. His plans had been going well; he had felt hopeful until just before curtain, when he happened to glance out into the audience.

Luckily, he had found this shack in the woods soon after coming to town; he thought he might need a place to stow things. At least he wasn't sleeping outdoors. But he was undecided. "Now what?" he kept saying, until the question had become a mantra that he heard in his mind, waking or sleeping. "Now what?"

Avery G. Prendergast drove absentmindedly along State Highway 55, periodically checking his watch and listening to the Cleveland Indians play the Chicago White Sox on XM Radio. He'd been glad to exchange the Fiesta for a larger, better-equipped rental, something he had done before leaving Lexington. From there, he had traveled to Bardstown and made a profitable deal on a Mary Todd Lincoln dress.

Now he was headed back to Hagan's Crossing. The next step would not be as easy; in fact, it might be rather unpleasant, but there was too much at stake to stop now.

He wondered if he had missed the turn he was supposed to make. "Damn GPS. Isn't it working?" He drove on for another half hour before deciding he needed to backtrack. By now, darkness was making the two-lane road feel more perilous as the local drivers impatiently sped around him. When he finally reached the junction with Highway 53, he said, "Yep, I missed it," and swung right. Checking his watch again, he saw that he still had plenty of time. The Indians were up by two in the seventh inning, he was still on schedule, and his mood lightened as he turned into the hotel parking lot.

For a June evening, it was not especially humid, and Franny sat on the front porch swing for a long time watching the lightning bugs emerge from the honeysuckle bushes and play hide-and- seek. That's how she had always thought of it as a child, that they would turn off their lights to hide, then reappear a few feet away for one bright second to say, "Go ahead, try to catch me."

Closing her eyes, she remembered the thrill of bare feet on the cool damp grass, chasing and jumping for the flickering lights just out of reach. The canning jar Mama gave her after punching holes in the top with a hammer and nail. She and Susan Watts from next door running back and forth across the yards in the magic darkness under the watchful eyes of their parents.

A cool breeze reminded her it was getting late, so she went in to get ready for bed. Franny had developed a nightly ritual that cured her of the insomnia that plagued her in her 70s. After a warm bath in a new walk-in tub, she put on a clean cotton gown, turned back the duvet, fluffed up her two down pillows, and sat in a chair she pulled up to the bed. She was long past being able to kneel, but she still said some night prayers.

Franny had been raised in the Episcopal Church. As a girl she'd been very devoted, although through much of her adulthood she had dismissed religion as unimportant. Now, in her old age, she had turned to look back and decided that in the absence of certainty, she would choose to believe in God because it gave her comfort and a connection to her parents. So she leaned upon the bed and recited the night prayer she had learned as a child: "Support us, Lord, all the day long, until the shadows lengthen and the evening comes, the busy world is hushed, the fever of life is over, and our work done; then, Lord, in your mercy, give us safe lodging, a holy rest, and peace at the last. Amen."

She prayed for the young man who had died, for his family, and for the person who had killed him. She prayed for Jesse; she thanked God for her health and the blessings of a comfortable home. Another prayer her mother had taught her sprang into memory: "Now I lay me down to sleep, I pray the Lord my soul to keep; If I should die before I wake, I pray the Lord my soul to take." *What a frightening idea to put into a little child's head at bedtime*, she thought. *How did I ever go to sleep, having been reminded I might not wake up?*

Franny found the iPod with her audiobooks. Then, settling comfortably in the bed and pulling the duvet up over her legs, she called Cecil several times. He didn't come. She thought he must be downstairs, so she took the cane she kept beside her bed and banged the floor three times so he could feel the vibrations.

"Cecil," she said when he finally came, "I think you're getting deaf like a little old man." He ran into the room and jumped up next to her. Actually, he climbed the three little stairs that she had placed near the foot of the bed because of his arthritic hips, but once on top of the covers, he jumped up and down a few times in excitement. Then he turned around in a circle several times before curling up in his spot next to her left hip.

Tonight she was listening to the end of *The Great Gatsby*. She set the sleep timer, turned off the light, glanced at the bedside clock—10:17—and closed her eyes. Often the soothing voice of the reader put her to sleep before the time ran out, but Franny could always backtrack the next evening. What she enjoyed most was listening to books she knew well, like a child who wants to hear the same story read every night at bedtime. She laughed at herself when she recognized how much she comforted herself with the rituals of childhood.

The fan in one of the open windows, set to low, and the ceiling fan above her bed combined to make a pleasing white noise, a backdrop for the cultured murmur of the narrator's voice:

> *Its vanished trees, the trees that had made way for Gatsby's house, had once pandered in whispers to the last and greatest of all human dreams; for a transitory enchanted moment man must have held his breath in the presence of this continent, compelled into an aesthetic contemplation he neither understood nor desired, face to face for the last time in history with something commensurate to his capacity for wonder.*
>
> *And as I sat there, brooding on the old unknown world, I thought of Gatsby's wonder when he first picked out the green light at the end of Daisy's dock. He had come a long way to this blue lawn and his dream must have seemed so close that he could hardly*

fail to grasp it. He did not know that it was already behind him, somewhere back in that vast obscurity beyond the city, where the dark fields of the republic rolled on under the night.

Gatsby believed in the green light, the orgiastic future that year by year recedes before us. It eluded us then, but that's no matter—tomorrow we will run faster, stretch out our arms farther. . . . And one fine morning—

So we beat on, boats against the current, borne back ceaselessly into the past.

Franny fell asleep before the final sentence.

—15—

What's Done Cannot Be Undone

The man carefully uncovered the acid-free archival box and sat down in front of it. Putting on cotton gloves, he reached into the box and lifted up a fragile piece of rag paper bearing faded cursive writing. It was obviously the left half of an old document, torn almost down the middle.

He could envision the document whole; in size, it had been perhaps seven by ten inches. It bore three distinct cursive styles, written in different inks, probably at different times. On the missing part, fragments of letters suggested there might also have been more writing.

The first inscription, at the top, said, "Sir, please accept this as a testament to your love of poetry and an expression of my wishes for your peace of mind and heart. EKS."

Beneath that were 13 lines of poetry. He had looked it up and discovered it was the beginning of the Keats poem *Endymion*. The last words of some lines were torn away, and the faded rusty brown ink was hard to read. He could only see a few letters on the lines written to the right of the poem—*N*, *lo*, *w*, *T*, *wo*, *Ken*, *bea*, *pall*, *gra*, and *ligh*—but the half signature at the bottom was clear. Since "pall" was an actual word in the Keats poem, he surmised that the missing writing was about the verse.

He held the paper in both hands reverently, like an offering, and thought about what he should do. He told himself he didn't have a choice. After an interval of about ten minutes, detailing the plan in his mind, he carefully returned the paper to its box and covered it as before.

Both Franny and Cecil snored a little, and the night was quiet, with the exception of an occasional train whistle from miles away. Franny unwittingly kicked away the duvet over her feet; Cecil shifted his position. Still, she slept soundly.

About 4:00 a.m., the birds in neighborhood trees began their morning song, but Franny did not hear them. Someone who did hear was a man dressed in black, who was at that moment carefully raising the screen of one of the open kitchen windows. He hoisted himself onto the sill and slipped through soundlessly.

For a long moment, he stood perfectly still in the dark kitchen until his eyes adjusted; then he walked stealthily into Jesse's room. Pulling out a small flashlight, he scanned the corners of the room and opened the closet door. Empty. Gliding down the long middle hallway like a ghost, he peered into each empty room before entering. He opened every closet.

Coming to the slightly open door of Franny's bedroom, he paused to listen for her rhythmic breathing. Through the door he could see moonlight reflected in the mirror above the washstand, casting an eerie shadow of the shimmering curtains, as though he had slipped through a tear in the fabric of time and stood at the threshold of his great-great-grandmother's boudoir.

He turned and moved on, up the uncarpeted stairs and down the long hall. Examining every room on the second floor in turn and not finding satisfaction, he was moving toward the front of the house to ascend to the third floor when he bumped into a table and a small bone-china lamp crashed to the floor.

He froze. Beads of sweat emerged on the sides of his forehead. He held his breath. He thought he heard a sound below. Had he awakened the old lady? Maybe not. Everything was quiet except for the ticking of a grandfather clock on the wide landing. He began to move on. But then came a scratching sound. *Oh damn*, he thought. A ratty little dog was scampering up the stairs. Seeing the intruder, Cecil began barking, yapping a high-pitched yap that would certainly wake the old lady. Just as the man in black grabbed at the dog, Cecil backed away from him into a bedroom and under the bed, still barking, and there was no way to reach him.

The intruder dropped to the floor and slid under the bed as far as he could, trying to grab Cecil by a foreleg. Cecil growled and bit at him and kept up the yapping. The man tried again, this time getting a firmer hold on the dog and sliding him all the way out into the center of the room.

"Damn, you're a squirmy little rat," the man said, trying to hold Cecil and grab a pillow to smother him. Cecil whined as loudly as he barked. Twisting himself out of the man's arms, he jumped to the floor and ran to the top of the steps. The intruder followed—and came face to face with Franny at the top of the stairs.

"You—" she said.

The man snarled, sounding like a larger species of dog. Cecil was running back and forth barking, growling, and snapping at the man, who with one kick of his right foot lifted the little dog into the air and launched him down the stairs.

Then he reached for Franny, who yelled, “Oh, no, you can’t—” and then seemed to lunge toward him. She lost her footing. He grabbed her upper arm, and she screamed. He let go.

She tumbled to the bottom of the steps and lay still.

16

The O'erfraught Heart

1841, FARMINGTON PLANTATION, KENTUCKY

Emma Speed walked out into the morning sunlight and gazed across the back garden, far into the fields of hemp. The August sun was already high in the sky, and the hazy tops of the plants wavered in the distant heat. "They look as if they are dancing," she said aloud to herself. All around her the plantation was bustling with activity: men loading a farm wagon, women making lye soap outside the detached kitchen, children weeding the garden.

August sunlight in Kentucky had a golden hue that dappled all the leaves of the garden plants and the row of azaleas along the walk. Emma mused about the conversation she had had with her husband's brother Joshua concerning his friend who was visiting from Springfield. She felt honored that Joshua had taken her into his confidence, but it occurred to her that he had talked to her to prevent her saying anything embarrassing to Mr. Lincoln. Joshua had specifically urged her not to mention anything about romance.

It saddened her to hear about Mr. Lincoln's struggle over the previous eight months, especially that he had become so low as to consider suicide. Joshua said that the melancholia had come upon Mr. Lincoln in January and that his friends had taken precautions to remove knives from his access. A friend had reported at the end of January that after three weeks of medical treatment by a Dr. Henry, Mr. Lincoln had emerged "reduced and emaciated." Over the succeeding months, Joshua had remained deeply concerned about his friend. Lincoln had written to Joshua, "I am now the most miserable man living," a phrase Emma had taken to heart.

Joshua had confided to his brother Philip that the young lawyer had suffered a loss in love. "What he needs is warm Kentucky sunshine, hearty Kentucky food, and the diversions of a large family. In short," he pronounced, "he needs Farmington." So it was that the invitation was extended and the family welcomed Mr. Lincoln.

Emma turned to the path leading around the house, thinking to take a solitary walk up the drive to the Louisville Road. With delight, she saw Mr. Lincoln a few strides ahead of her, having come down the front steps with apparently the same purpose.

"Mr. Lincoln."

At the sound of his name, he turned and made a slight bow.

"Mrs. Speed, why, how handsome you look on this beautiful morning."

Only 17, and two months married, Emma blushed at being called "Mrs." so gallantly by the tall, lanky Mr. Lincoln. He was decidedly not handsome, she thought, and in the weeks he had been a houseguest—lodged in a bedroom down the hall from her own—he had sometimes looked so deeply sad that his countenance was alarming. Today, however, his mood seemed lighter.

Mr. Lincoln waited now at the base of the steps, and in a moment, Emma was at his side.

"I was going to take a walk before the day gets too hot," she said.

"As was I," he replied. "May I accompany you?" He gestured toward the long driveway lined with locust and walnut trees.

She smiled in response, and they began walking in silence.

Emma knew that Mr. Lincoln had been born in Kentucky, to a farming family of much more modest means than the Speeds, and that he was a lawyer who had served in the Illinois legislature. That his table manners were as rough-hewn as his visage was also evident; Philip's Aunt Mildred had declared she was appalled when he set the jelly bowl next to his own plate after it was handed to him, as if he had never eaten mutton at a formal dinner table in his 32 years! Then, seeing others pass the jelly around the table, Lincoln had questioned Joshua. Joshua's answer was that he had expected Lincoln to watch what he did and follow suit! Aunt Mildred had sniffed her disapproval of Joshua's houseguest.

Emma herself did not find fault with Mr. Lincoln's lack of social graces; being young, she thought the older generation put too much store in appearances. Her upbringing in Louisville with two parents raised in England—her father having become an influential man of business and courted in literary circles because of his famous brother, the poet John Keats—lay somewhere between the poverty of the Lincolns and the privilege of the Speeds. She felt an affinity toward Mr. Lincoln, with a touch of protectiveness.

Mr. Lincoln cleared his throat. Called back to the present, Emma was aware that the silence seemed to render him nervous and awkward, not like the gallant man who had just greeted her. He glanced away, then cleared his throat again, as if he were mounting an effort to speak.

She spoke instead. "The dinner we had last night was most enjoyable."

"Yes, indeed it was. I am not accustomed to such elegance. I hope I did not embarrass myself," Lincoln replied.

"Oh, no, of course not, Mr. Lincoln. Why, I thought your comments in the discussion of the need for broader education were very well received by the Unitarian minister, Mr. Heywood. He is quite a learned man and a great proponent of public education, and I saw he nodded with enthusiasm when you spoke."

"You're very kind, Mrs. Speed."

"Please, do call me Emma."

"I shall call you 'Aunt Emma,'" he said, "because you have won the hearts of the children.

They never tire of your affectionate attention."

"They can be quite rambunctious, can they not, running and playing hide-and-seek in the hallways?" she asked.

Lincoln agreed, laughing about the rowdy play of a recent evening and claiming that he had been the intended object of Miss Mary Speed's potential assault and battery, resulting in the necessity of shutting her up in a room. Lincoln expressed his enjoyment of being welcomed into Joshua's large, happy family, in contrast to his being alone, before he met Joshua, and as poor as Job's turkey.

"My coming into Joshua's store was undoubtedly fortuitous. He has become a most"— Lincoln hesitated—"a most enduring friend to me."

Emma nodded and encouraged Mr. Lincoln to talk about their lives in Springfield. He described the contrast between the simplicity of living above the general store, two men living a spartan bachelor existence, and the comforts of living at Farmington.

"I suppose you have had very little experience of being waited on by Negro servants," Emma said.

"I have had none, none at all. I confess I do not find it a comfortable experience."

This caused an awkward pause in the conversation, as Emma felt she had led him to say something slightly critical of his hosts, and he seemed to have become ill at ease again. This was an opportune time to mention the subject she genuinely wanted to broach.

The previous evening, Joshua had teased Mr. Lincoln about being an aspiring poet, which Emma could see had embarrassed him. At the time, she had felt cross with Joshua, and at bedtime she had complained to her husband, "I just do not understand the nature of male friendships, Philip, why you deride one another and seem to enjoy inflicting such mortification. A woman would never treat her dearest friend that way."

"Yes, Emma, my dear," he said, kissing her on the forehead, "but men wear their feelings differently."

Philip had fallen asleep quickly, but Emma had lain awake thinking. Hearing his measured breathing, she had slid from the bed, tiptoed across the room, lifted a folded sheet of paper from her Bible, and tucked it into the reticule she would carry the next day.

Now Emma slipped her hand into the reticule. She went on talking.

"Mr. Lincoln, last evening I was pleased hearing of your interest in poetry. Do you have any favorites?"

"Yes, I suppose I do. There is one poem I like exceedingly, although I do not know its author. I have memorized it:

O why should the spirit of mortal be proud?
Like a fast-flitting meteor, a fast-flying cloud,
A flash of the lightning, a break of the wave,
He passes from life to his rest in the grave.

"That is only the first stanza—I will not go on. It is a poem on the brevity of life."

"As much poetry properly is," Emma said. She paused. "Mr. Lincoln, I think Joshua was cruel to tease you last evening. Of course, you know I think poetry a fine calling. My uncle, John Keats, whom my father so dearly loved, might have been a great poet had he lived. As it was, he composed many poems which my father maintains are as good as those of Shelley or Wordsworth."

Lincoln grimaced. "You should not mention my poor verses in the same breath as the names of Keats, Shelley, and Wordsworth, Miss Emma. That constitutes literary blasphemy." He smiled.

Emma had stopped walking and turned to face him. Removing the paper and unfolding it, she handed it to him, saying, "Nevertheless, Mr. Lincoln, I should like to give this to you, as an inspiration and a token of friendship."

He opened the handwritten paper and read aloud.

A thing of beauty is a joy for ever:
Its loveliness increases; it will never
Pass into nothingness; but still will keep
A bower quiet for us, and a sleep
Full of sweet dreams, and health, and quiet breathing.
Therefore, on every morrow, are we wreathing
A flowery band to bind us to the earth,

Spite of despondence, of the inhuman dearth
Of noble natures, of the gloomy days,
Of all the unhealthy and o'er-darkened ways
Made for our searching: yes, in spite of all,
Some shape of beauty moves away the pall
From our dark spirits.

They were both silent.

"I am deeply moved, Miss Emma." It was almost a whisper. "I am sorry that I do not recognize the lines; are they—"

"My uncle's," she said. "These are the opening lines from *Endymion*, a pastoral romance he wrote in 1818. My father says that Uncle John was excoriated in some of the reviews, and he felt it keenly; it broke his heart. It was a setback, but I think he honestly believed what he wrote— that beauty supersedes all and raises us up."

She paused.

"This is a page he sent my father in 1817. And I hope, Mr. Lincoln, that you will do me the honor of recording your thoughts on the lines. I would appreciate knowing your"—she hesitated—"feelings."

He glanced down, his visage darkened, and for a moment Emma thought she had spoken too boldly. But then he looked at her, and she saw the warmth in his eyes.

"Thank you, ma'am. I am most heartily grateful and honored." He refolded the paper and placed it in his pocket. Then he offered her his arm, and they began to walk again in companionable silence back toward the house.

Genealogy of the Speed Family (Partial)

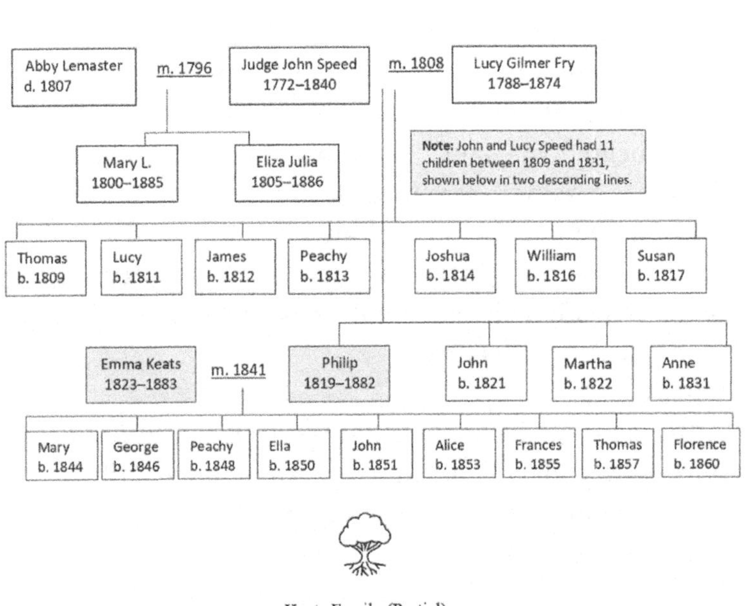

Keats Family (Partial)

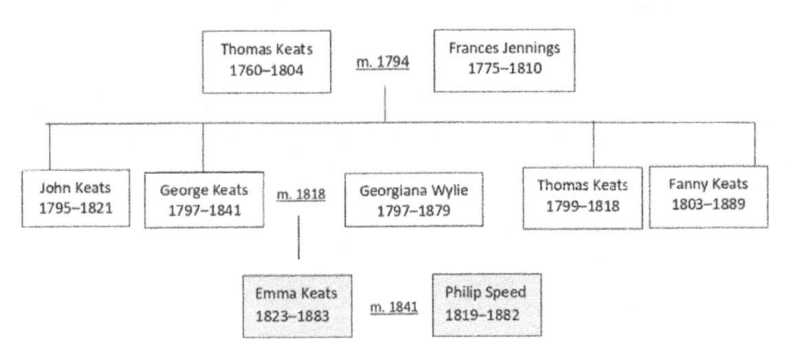

–17–

Look like th' Innocent Flower

Maggie's research in the trunks on Sunday had answered some of her questions and raised a dozen more. Monday morning found her at the local historical society, which was housed in an old Carnegie library, repurposed after the county built a larger, more modern structure equipped for the digital age. The Carnegie building had cool marble stairs and brass railings that Maggie had loved since she was a little girl getting her first library card and taking out her first book, *A Little Maid of Mohawk Valley,* part of a series about young heroines in the War of Independence.

First she went to the 19th-century maps and located the site on the river where the Endymion plantation house had been built. Then she searched for the deed to the property, confirming Marshall's account that a man named Rankin sold it to the Speeds. Philip Speed bought it in 1843 with a partially built house. The property remained in Speed hands until 1879. Then ownership remained in a trust until the property was purchased in 1920. Maggie examined the deed of sale.

"Oh, that's interesting," she said. She took a photo of the document with her cell phone.

From the deeds room, she went to the photographic archives and located folders on prominent families. She found George Keats as a young man with an aquiline nose, full lips, and a receding hairline. The backdrop of the painting was a white cloud with blue sky showing in the upper left, an artistic touch which made the most of his being a poet's brother.

Judge John Speed, looking about 50, wore a heavy brown coat with the collar raised in back, a white shirt, and a cravat tied tightly at the neck. His long, stern face and slight hook nose were made less serious by his eyeglasses, perched above his forehead. Lucy Speed, the mother of Philip, James, and Joshua Fry Speed, was depicted in a white lace bonnet and round lace bib that framed her head and face like a halo. Maggie found a double portrait of Abraham Lincoln and Joshua Fry Speed in middle age, labeled "Friendship," and a picture of Franny's great- grandfather, Isaac Caldwell Jr., Esq., with a large law book open in his hands. His countenance was marked by bushy eyebrows and a strong chin.

There must have been two dozen smaller photographs of enslaved people, one a daguerreotype of two men, three women, and two children dressed in rags in front of a small cabin, another a formal portrait of a Black couple in fine attire, he in a black frock coat, she in a beribboned bonnet.

There were pictures of men and women surrounded by hemp, women stirring large cauldrons of boiling water, mothers with nursing babies, and most disturbing of all, a chain of half-naked men shackled at their ankles and wrists being prodded up a ramp onto a riverboat for sale elsewhere. She studied the faces, wondering if one of the women might be Cassie or one of the men Joseph.

Maggie found a comprehensive genealogical chart for the

Speeds going back to John Speed, an historian and cartographer born in England in 1552. She took in the surnames that repeated throughout the generations as middle names: Rankin, Fry, Keats, Gilmer, and Smith. At first glance, she read Gilmer as Gilemorane and got excited, but then she realized her mistake.

From another folder, she withdrew a watercolor sketch of an octagonal home with a wide river in the background and tall cottonwood trees on either side. She knew immediately this was Endymion. On the back of the drawing, Maggie found the description:

> *Endymion, octagonal home of Philip Speed and Emma Keats Speed, built in 1846 as a summer retreat. Basement: office, billiard room, school room, and caretaker's quarters. Principal floor: hall, reception room, drawing room, breakfast room, dining room, library, and music room, four verandas. Second floor: hall, gallery, four bed chambers, dressing rooms. The center cupola allows light to enter from above. Dedicated to the memory of John Keats 1795 –1821, the home features many allusions to his poetry, including carved nightingales and wreaths of white hawthorn, eglantine, violets, and musk -roses topping the pillars. The center window of each triplet is etched at its top with a Grecian urn. The gardens around the house were planted with peonies, morning r oses, poppies, and fruit trees. On the lintel above the front door was carved "A thing of beauty is a joy for ever; its loveliness increases; it will never pass into nothingness."*

In the same folder Maggie found a photograph of the Speed house at Farmington, showing the stone bridge across Beargrass Creek and the long driveway approaching the red-brick structure. A brief notation read: *Abraham Lincoln visited here in the summer of 1841 with his best friend Joshua Speed.*

Surrounded by all the photos, Maggie sat for a long while peering into the faces of the white slave owners and the Blacks they had enslaved. They gazed back at her imperturbably.

"A thing of beauty," she said aloud, "will not pass into nothingness, Mr. Keats, but neither will the marks of pain or the weight of suffering."

The watercolor of Endymion kept drawing her eye back to its white balconies and crowning cupola. She could envision Emma Keats Speed looking down on the garden, watching a Black man on his knees weeding among what her uncle had described in his "Ode on Melancholy" as a "wealth of globed peonies." Endymion held the key to a mystery, Maggie knew. Then, underneath the watercolor, she found even more interesting items, a set of yellowed clippings without the newspaper's name. The date 1874 was handwritten in the corner:

A DARING ROBBERY
A PARTY OF ARMED AND MASKED ROBBERS
BREAK INTO A HOUSE AT NIGHT
Prominent Personages Victimized
in Inexplicable Burglary
Family Papers Stolen
Negro Servant Killed

The brazenness of ruffians in our cities and rural areas was once again illustrated in a recent burglary that took place on Thursday evening at a plantation home in northern Oldham County. Fantastic imaginings have been circulated among the local population, constructing theories about the perpetrators and their possible motives.

Sometime on the night of Thursday last, an unknown number of burglars gained entry into the lavishly furnished plantation home Endymion, owned by Major Philip Speed and his wife Emma Keats Speed. The office on the lower level of the three-story home was the scene of chaos and destruction. Three desks had been ransacked. Evidence of the desks being pried open included a new screw - driver with a chipped edge found on the floor. Every drawer bore the marks of being broken open; papers were rummaged through and cast onto the floor.

A safe was also pried open and its contents rifled through. Apparently, cash, bonds, and personal papers were taken. On the second floor of the house, where is it believed that the robbers entered, burlap bags of silver goblets, trays, and candlesticks were abandoned. Most disturbingly, a Negro servant of the family, Joseph Clark, who had been with the Speeds since before the war, was found dead on the floor. It is assumed that he surprised the intruders and was coldly dispatched.

Detective Harris Oakley visited the scene and questioned those present on the night of the robbery. The caretaker, who identified himself as "Mr. Elijah" and who lives on the property, informed Detective Oakley that st rangers had been seen trekking through the nearby woods the day before, casti ng some suspicion that the robbery was perpetrated by thieves who are well away by now. Sources close to Oakley say there are many unanswered questions.

The caretaker objected to Detective Oakley's insistence on sealing off the vandalized room until the Speeds could return. Insisting that he needed to clean up the scattered papers, the man became quite belligerent and only relented when he was threatened with arrest. The room was sealed.

The burglary took place sometime between one o'clock a.m. and six o'clock a.m., according to the testimony of the caretaker. The Speeds themselves were visiting friends in upstate New York and were notified of the loss by telegram the next day.

The investigation will continue in hopes of determining what was taken and by whom.

Maggie read the brief article three times. The theft of papers was intriguing. She knew this Joseph Clark had to be Cassie's husband, Mary Lou's great-grandfather. So the family story of his having been murdered was true—and maybe this robbery was connected to the so-called treasure.

She found a second clipping:

VALUED KEATS LETTERS AND POEMS AMONG STOLEN PAPERS

Following an inventory of the papers remaining after the infamous Endymion robbery, Mrs. Emma Keats Speed has confirmed that among the items stolen were personal letters from her uncle, the English poet John Keats, to her now -deceased father, George Keats. It was the custom of the Keats brothers to exchange long letters composed over an interval of time, covering the events of a fortnight, and containing

> much personal reflection. John Keats often enclosed hand-written copies of his poetry, some of which was unpublished. Mrs. Speed was said to be distraught at the loss of some particular poems in her uncle's hand. When asked to comment, she demurred, saying only that the loss was too personal.

After making copies of the articles, Maggie gathered her materials and decided to walk to the courthouse three blocks away. The sun was bright, and the glare on the white limestone and marble buildings along Main Street made Maggie wish she had brought her sunglasses. It wasn't worth a walk back to the car, though, since there was plenty of shade. On each block, between the sidewalk and the street, 70-year-old maple trees spaced 20 feet apart formed a lush canopy. As Maggie got closer to the courthouse, foot traffic picked up, and she nodded a hello to several passing acquaintances.

Inside the county records office, Maggie easily found the deed books. The room was crowded with paralegals tracing property rights and liens for real estate attorneys, but she found a corner where she could conduct her search. She was pleased with the result.

"This is curiouser and curiouser," Maggie said aloud.

18

Their Exits and Their Entrances

On her way home from the courthouse, Maggie was feeling jubilant. The idea that something of value—something stolen from Endymion—might be at the root of a mystery seemed plausible. Now she decided to stop by Franny Babcock's to check on her.

Just as she was about to turn onto Woodbine, Maggie had to pull the car over.

She saw Franny in her garden happily gathering an armful of blue, white, and purple hydrangeas, Cecil at her heel, bounding in the grass. Franny looked up and raised the brim of her sunhat slightly, speaking words of welcome, although Maggie heard no sound. Franny cradled the hydrangeas in the crook of her left arm and extended her right hand as if to walk Maggie up the white steps onto the porch. Maggie had never seen her look so happy.

The image was gone in an instant, but Maggie found it unsettling.

"I think I'm meant to check on her," she said aloud.

She parked in front of Franny's house, and although the afternoon was heating up, she stood for a moment admiring Franny's garden, especially the blue hydrangeas thick enough to spill over the porch railing.

She knocked several times and waited, peering through one of the sidelights. It was hard to see through the lace curtains. Knocking again, she called loudly, "Franny! Franny? Are you here?" She heard Cecil whining. She went to the other sidelight, closer to where Cecil was—and thought she could see something on the floor.

She recognized the figure of Franny Babcock lying sprawled at the foot of the stairs.

"Oh Franny, no, oh Franny," Maggie cried.

She phoned Jimmy Callahan and described what she saw.

He cursed, then told her to hold tight; he would be there in 10 minutes.

Maggie sat on the glider on the porch, exactly where she had sat on Friday alongside Franny. Every few minutes she would go back to look in the window, hoping she had imagined the scene or misunderstood, but Franny lay perfectly still, Cecil lying a foot away. Maggie felt a terrible sadness, and she wanted to hear Jack's voice. She called his cell phone. It rang, but when it went to voice mail, she hung up and put the phone on silent. She moved her car from the driveway to the street to make room for the ambulance and returned to the front porch.

When Callahan arrived, he jimmied the door open and he and Maggie entered the foyer. Maggie rushed to Franny. Callahan yelled, "Stop! Don't touch anything!" Maggie said, "I won't," but she knelt by the body and touched her fingertips to Franny's arm. Stone cold. Franny was lying on her back with her left leg tucked under her right leg, arms slightly outstretched, and head facing away from the stairs. It seemed as if she had fallen down the stairs backward. Blood had pooled under the back of her head. Cecil whimpered in obvious pain and tried to get to his feet but couldn't.

"Jimmy, can I take care of Cecil? I know this is a crime scene, but he's suffering," Maggie asked.

"Yes—just get him out of the way," Jimmy said, "without touching anything else."

Maggie found the carrier in the kitchen and tried to pick up Cecil, who growled but finally let her get hold of him. As she picked him up, he whined and relieved himself.

"Oh, poor baby." She took him into the kitchen, away from Franny's body.

Callahan did a walk-through of the house and returned to the foyer. Within minutes, the group heard approaching sirens. An ambulance and a patrol car pulled up in front of the house. The county medical examiner came with the forensics team. Callahan directed patrolmen to search the perimeter of the house to see if there had been a break-in. Maggie thought about calling Danny to come and get the dog, but that would have to wait.

Maggie answered Callahan's questions about why she had come to Franny's, what time she had arrived, and what she had seen. It surprised her how detached she felt. She watched the crime investigators take photos from every angle and turn Franny's body to examine the wound at the back of her head. They measured the distance between her feet and the base of the stairs, checked the stairs for blood, and dusted for fingerprints.

With everything documented, they put Franny's body into a bag; hearing the sound of the zipper triggered Maggie's tears. Franny had been frightened by the man in the maroon car and the man who demanded to see the documents. And it looked as if she really had been in danger.

I didn't take this seriously enough, Maggie thought. *Oh, Franny, I'm sorry.*

When the body had been removed, Callahan asked Maggie to walk through the house with him to see if she recognized anything missing. They went from room to room on the first and second floors, but Maggie didn't notice anything out of place.

"I really haven't been through the house in a long time, Jimmy, so I can't be sure, but there are plenty of small items of value still here, like these," she said, picking up a porcelain figure from a marble-topped table.

"This set of Meissen figurines of commedia dell'arte characters is probably 18th century— and worth thousands of dollars. I guess what I notice most is what the intruder didn't take. Over there, on the mantelpiece, those silver candlesticks are George III, sterling, worth at least $5,000. It doesn't seem like much of a robbery," Maggie said.

"Geez, I didn't know she had so much money," Callahan said.

"Well, it was mostly in the antiques she had inherited," Maggie said.

The officers who had searched the yard came to report finding one of the kitchen windows open, with the screen removed. A bench on the back porch had been dragged in front of the open window, and inside the kitchen, a bottle of dishwashing liquid looked as if it had been knocked into the sink, leaving a pool of blue soap.

"We closed the windows on the first floor," the officer said. "What about the dog?"

"Oh hell," Callahan said.

"Could one of your officers take him to Danny to get him checked out?" Maggie asked. "He needs medical care."

"All right, then." He nodded to the officer holding the dog carrier. "Let's seal the doors and follow up with the morgue." He gave Maggie a sideways hug.

"I heard back from Baldwin College," Callahan added to Maggie. "They have no record of a Jesse Gilemorane ever attending, much less graduating. So he must have lied to Erik."

Maggie's blue eyes took on a steely look. She could feel anger rising in her.

"Well, I couldn't find a probable family of Gilemoranes in Kentucky or Ohio, so I think you're right about that."

"Oh, and I got the results on Ron Spear," Callahan said. He explained that the autopsy showed death was caused by a solution of sodium cyanide dissolved in a solvent called DMSO and absorbed into the ear. Both the cyanide and the DMSO could have been purchased over the internet, and so far he had no means of tracking the source.

He said he had scanned the lengthy pathology report, which indicated that the cyanide had traveled through the eustachian tube into the larynx and been aspirated. He didn't understand every phrase, but he could recognize from past cases that "dark cyanotic hypostasis," "lack of oxygenation of the red cells," and "paralysis of the respiratory muscle" added up to cyanide poisoning and murder. The concentration of the cyanide was serious enough to put the pathologist at some risk during the autopsy.

"Whoever prepared the vial of poison wasn't leaving much to chance," he finished.

Maggie wiped away tears and said, "Jimmy, I wonder if the two deaths are connected."

"Dunno. Sorry you've had to go through this, Maggie. Wait a minute—did Miss Babcock have any relatives I should contact?" Maggie said she didn't know. Callahan said he would send someone later in the day to search for personal records.

Meanwhile, Maggie saw that the police were not going to clean up Franny's blood. Gathering paper towels and wood floor cleaner from the kitchen, Maggie knelt where Franny had lain and wiped up the dried blood, scrubbing to erase what had soaked into the oak floorboards. *It will need professional cleaning*, she thought.

Everyone else went out the front door, and Maggie followed. One by one they drove away, leaving Maggie sitting alone in her car. She felt she could not leave. She sat there for most of an hour, thinking, running through the list of the items she had found the day before in the trunks.

There had been lots of legal correspondence she had only skimmed. She had found a yellowed circular announcing two runaway slaves, offering a $100 reward. Their descriptions had featured the marks of cruelty. One man was identifiable because he was missing two fingers and had scars on his cheekbone and left arm from dog bites. The other man had a back "badly scarred from the whip." Just underneath the notice she'd found pieces of a large copy of the Emancipation Proclamation, torn in half, then torn in half again.

That a copy of this particular document lay hidden in the

dark for all these decades just under the advertisement for runaway slaves had struck Maggie as a bitter irony. In those trunks lay the hidden struggles of hundreds of forgotten people whose stories would never be told. Those who died in slavery, those whose descendants didn't—and couldn't—realize what they had endured: the remnants of so many lives.

She thought about Mary Lou's family at Farmington and about Emma Keats and Philip Speed. It was so curious that they had known Lincoln.

She thought about the Endymion robbery and murder she had read about this morning. It had involved a theft of documents, with other valuables overlooked. That too seemed strangely coincidental. Did Franny die for the same reason as Mary Lou's great-grandfather?

A fragment of Keats that she had read the night before popped into her mind: "Now more than ever seems it rich to die, to cease upon the midnight with no pain."

Maggie's eyes brimmed with tears, but she took a deep breath and calmed herself. She decided that before she left, she wanted to walk around the back of the house to see where the intruder had gotten in. Just as she was rounding the corner into the back yard, she was stunned to see a young man opening the back door with a key.

They stared at one another like a *tableau vivant.*

19

At One Fell Swoop

1846, FARMINGTON PLANTATION, KENTUCKY

Athena heard the bell that rang every morning at 4:00 a.m. and stirred under the patchwork quilt, but she did not open her eyes. If she kept her eyes shut, she could hope for a few more minutes of warmth, as if not seeing others get up from their corn shuck mattresses could make it not so. She felt a poke in the back.

"Git up now; you ain't gonna lie-a-bed. Us gotta get movin'."

The voice belonged to another enslaved woman, Macy, who was in her 40s, at least 20 years older than Athena.

"You young folk gonna get the boss man in a bad mood with your lazin' 'round. And us all be payin' the price."

Athena pulled the cover back and reluctantly stood in the dark cabin. It was a chilly morning in April. Someone was stoking the banked fire with little success. Athena pulled her cotton dress over the coarse linen shift she never removed and hurriedly splashed water on her face from the bucket near the door. She had less than 20 minutes to eat some cornbread and a small piece of hogback, which would have to hold her through to midday.

One of her jobs was milking the cows and carrying the

heavy pails of milk to the spring house, where the milk could be cooled. Athena and several other women then drove the cows out into the pasture. They would need to be retrieved later in the day for a second milking. Athena would also make cheese and butter from the milk.

Stepping out of the cabin, Athena looked toward the big house and wondered about her child Cassie. Nearly five years old, Cassie had been taken to live in the big house as a baby, nearly as soon as she could walk. At first, it was just an occasional event: one of the white folks would see the toddler and show an interest. But then the mistress, Lucy Speed, and her daughters Miss Mary and Miss Eliza had practically snatched her up. Cassie looked almost as white as anyone in the family, and they had taken to dressing her up in fancy dresses like a miniature lady. Her eyes were brown and wide as saucers. Her dark brown hair wasn't nappy at all, and curled in ringlets it made her look like a doll. That's what they had done, taken her baby girl and turned her into a doll for the white ladies to play with. Now she was kept in the big house all the time, and they didn't even acknowledge that Athena was her mother.

Cassie's birth was traumatic; Athena labored for 18 hours and lost a deal of blood. She was given three weeks to recover, and because she was so weak, another enslaved woman with an infant was given Cassie to nurse. Athena wasn't even able to feed her child.

Anger rose up in her as her mind went back to the night of the rape. A white man—she did not even know which one—came into the cabin where she lay sleeping, and before she knew what was happening, he was on top of her. The scent of bourbon and tobacco on his breath, mixed with the odor of his body and hair, turned her stomach. When

Cassie was born, Macy said she was a curse and that Athena should hope the baby's skin would darken. Some of the other women looked on her with contempt. "We don't need no bright Negroes round here," Macy said. The one who doted the most on Cassie was Miss Emma Speed. She and her husband had been living at Farmington for two years before Cassie was born. They had married just after Judge Speed had died and Mr. Joshua had returned to the plantation. *Things is so complicated with them white folk*, Athena thought. Sometimes she wished she could work in the big house so she could see her baby, but she didn't particularly like to deal with the ladies of the house. It seemed they couldn't do anything for themselves. They'd say, "Pour me a glass of tea," and expect a Negro woman to walk across the room to do it, even if the pitcher was five inches from their own hand. They were all smiles and sweetness talking to their menfolk but sharp-tongued with the cook or the housemaids.

Every day Athena would watch for Miss Emma to bring Cassie outside to walk or play in the shade under the wide oak trees. Miss Emma had given Cassie a miniature pink parasol just like her own and had dresses made for her with crinolines and petticoats. She had even given her a doll dressed the same way. It was strange, Athena thought. Cassie was the image of Miss Emma, and the doll was the image of Cassie.

Cassie had once known that Athena was her ma, but Athena did not know whether Cassie remembered that now; they had been kept apart for the better part of three years. On the rare occasion that Cassie might be standing alone in the yard, Athena would stop in her work and stand perfectly still, gazing at her, saying under her breath, "Look here, chile, lookee here at me."

Once Cassie did see Athena and began running away from the house toward her as she was herding the cows to pasture. In a moment, Miss Emma came flying out the back door, caught Cassie up in her arms, and carried her inside. Athena could not stop the tears.

For some time now, there had been talk that Mr. Philip and Miss Emma were going to move from Farmington to a house they had built up on the Ohio River. Athena always listened carefully if the topic came up within earshot. She was hoping Miss Emma would move away right soon so that maybe Cassie would not be kept in the big house anymore. Miss Emma already had a little girl of her own, Mary Eliza, and a baby boy, George. Athena wished she would spend her energy doting on them.

On this day, just after the midday meal was served in the big house, some large wagons came up the drive and pulled around to the back of the house. Housemaids and porters began carrying out chests and boxes of all sizes, and the whisper went through the kitchen and into the larder where Athena was churning butter: "They's loadin' up the wagons. Looks like they's goin' today."

Athena didn't dare leave the churn to go and watch, as the butter had just begun to gather, but she was so distracted that she kept losing her rhythm. As she was close to finished she heard someone call out, "They's goin'."

She dropped the paddle and ran to the yard, where the household had gathered. Her excitement turned to fear as she saw one of the nursemaids carrying Cassie out the back door and toward Miss Emma, seated in a carriage that had been drawn up behind the wagons. A second carriage held the other Speed children and a nursemaid.

Without thinking, Athena bolted from the group of slaves, calling out, "Cassie! Cassie! No! Don't take my chile." Reaching the pair, she tried to wrestle Cassie from the nurse's arms, still calling her name over and over. Mr. Philip, who had not yet entered the carriage, grabbed Athena from behind, pulling her away. Cassie was now crying loudly. Miss Emma leaned out of the coach, saying, "Give me the child—give her to me now." The nurse lifted Cassie onto Miss Emma's lap and backed away. Mr. Philip remonstrated with Athena, "Now then, control yourself. The child does not belong to you."

"Please, sir, please don't take her away from me. She is my baby, she is. Oh Lord, Lord help me, I can't stand if you take her away!" While she said these words, Athena struggled to turn around to address him, but his grip on her arms was too tight. He nodded to the overseer who was approaching.

"Take her. Make her see sense," he said.

The overseer stepped up and struck Athena a hard blow across the face, then grabbed her arms as Philip Speed let go. Not even looking back, Speed strode to the open carriage door and took his seat beside his wife. Cassie was still crying and being shushed by Miss Emma. Philip waved to his mother and sisters.

Within minutes, the wagons, the carriage, and Athena's baby girl Cassie were leaving Farmington for good.

Athena collapsed onto the ground, wailing out her sorrow. She didn't hear the overseer's threats; she endured the lashing she received in punishment for her outburst, and she lay senseless on the ground for six hours afterward. No one was allowed to carry her to the cabin.

In the days and weeks following, Athena grew more and more insolent and intractable. She stopped eating and moved about in slow motion, often seeming not to hear when she was spoken to. Punishment had no effect on her. Finally the decision was made to sell her in the slave market in Louisville. "She's not worth her keep," the overseer had said to Mrs. Speed. "She's jest poisoning the whole lot of them with her orneriness."

And so, a month after Cassie was taken from her, Athena was sold down the river to Louisiana to pick cotton.

20

Too Dear for my Possessing

The young man stood perfectly still, staring at Maggie in obvious panic.

"Who are you?" Maggie demanded. "What are you doing? Why are you going into Franny's house?"

She realized she had left her phone in the car. If she ran to get it, he might get away.

"Tell me," she practically yelled at him. "Tell me who you are."

"Jesse. I'm Jesse. I live here."

"You're the missing actor?" Maggie said. "Franny was worried sick about you. Where have you been?"

"Why is that your business? Who are you?" Jesse asked.

Maggie recognized him now from the playbill photo, and she softened her voice. His sandy- brown hair was cut close, thicker on top and shorter on the sides, giving him an artsy look. He looked as if he had been roughing it, his jeans muddied and torn. His cotton T-shirt was dirty as well, stained with something that looked like oil. She noted that he had not shaved in a couple of days, and his brown eyes looked bloodshot beneath his furrowed brow.

"I'm sorry. My name is Maggie O'Malley. I'm a friend of Franny's—well—"

"I've come back to get some things I left in the attic. Franny can explain who I am."

"Something has happened, Jesse. Franny isn't here. Would you let me in? I'll tell you about it."

He sat down on a kitchen chair when Maggie came in.

"Something happened, you said. Did something happen to Franny? Is she all right?"

His concern seemed genuine. If he was involved in Franny's death, Maggie thought, he was a better actor than Erik thought.

Maggie sat down.

"No. No, she's not. Franny's dead."

"Dead? Oh God, no. What happened?"

"They don't know the cause of death." Maggie decided not to give away too much information.

"Did someone break into the house? Was there a robbery?"

"Why do you ask that? What do you think might be missing?" she asked. She wondered if he would mention the trunks and papers—if, in fact, he knew they were gone.

"I dunno. I just can't believe this, unless it was—"

"Unless it was who?" Maggie asked.

Jesse didn't answer.

Maggie's mind was swirling with thoughts and feelings. She didn't want Jesse to get away; she wanted Jimmy to come walking around the corner. Anger welled up as she pictured Franny on the floor and thought of Jesse hiding somewhere when he might have been there to help her.

Jesse stared at the floor. He had sounded as if he were choked up. She didn't necessarily believe that Jesse had pushed Franny down the stairs, but she didn't really know him. She only knew what Franny had told her, that he was a "nice young man," and Franny could have been taken in.

"When did she die?" Jesse asked.

"Last night, probably. Or maybe early this morning."

They sat silently for a half a minute. Maggie was wondering how she could get Jesse to go with her to Jimmy.

"Do you know what happened to Ron Spear?"

"Yeah, that was terrible. Ron was a good guy."

"Can you explain what happened?"

"No. It's complicated."

"Why did you leave the park?"

He ignored the question.

"I just don't understand why you left the park," she said.

He shifted as if he were going to stand up, and most of all, Maggie wanted to keep him talking. She softened her voice. "You look like you've had a rough time."

"Yeah, I've been keeping out of sight since last Thursday, trying to figure out what to do."

"Are you in danger?"

He ignored the question.

"Where have you been for the past four nights?"

Eyes fixed on the floor, Jesse shook his head.

"I read your bio in the Shakespeare Festival playbill," she said. "You mentioned coming home to your roots or something like that. Your family was from Hagan's Crossing?"

"My grandparents. I grew up in Ohio."

"So you don't know anyone in town?"

Jesse ignored this question too. Instead he started talking

about how good Franny had been to him, how welcoming, how much he had enjoyed her cooking and her company.

"She was like a grandmother."

"Yes, she was," Maggie said. "And she absolutely loved Cecil, didn't she?" Maggie went into a description of Franny's affection for Cecil. Then, feigning ignorance, she looked around and said, "I haven't heard Cecil. I wonder where he is . . ."

"Well, he was—"

"He was what?"

"Um, probably they took him away."

"They?" she asked.

"The police—or whoever found Franny," Jesse said. He wouldn't meet her eyes.

"Had Franny known your grandmother who came from here?" Maggie asked.

"Um, no. I mean, I'm not sure; I never asked her. It didn't come up," Jesse said.

"That seems odd. Franny had a lot of curiosity. It's bizarre that she wouldn't have grilled you on your family connections. By the way, what was your grandmother's name?"

"Abigail Gilemorane," he said.

Maggie knitted her brow.

"When did you graduate from college?"

"Last December. Why are you asking these questions?"

"I'm just trying to get to know you."

An awkward silence settled, during which he repeatedly squeezed his left hand with his right as if he were trying to wring the water out of a rag. His hands were trembling as well, and beads of sweat formed at his hairline.

Maggie noticed how often Jesse's eyes cut to the door.

"Do you know what happened to Franny?" Jesse asked.

"No," Maggie said flatly. "No, I don't."

Maggie decided to take a chance.

"Listen to me. You've obviously in some kind of trouble. Franny genuinely cared about you, and she would want you to be safe. I think that if you went with me to see Chief Callahan, he could protect you from whatever danger is worrying you. No one is blaming you for anything that has happened."

Maggie realized she was saying all of this in the tone of voice one uses to calm a frightened animal. She felt for a moment that Jesse was being persuaded. A stifled sob escaped; he held his breath and looked at his hands.

"Please tell me what's going on. I want to help," Maggie said.

He began fighting the tears, holding his breath and wiping his eyes alternately with the backs of his hands.

"Why did you leave the park Thursday night?

Were you threatened?" A look of terror flashed in his eyes. "I can't. I can't. I have to go."

He bolted from the chair and shot out the back door in a matter of seconds.

"Damn," Maggie said out loud. She followed to the porch and around to the front of the house, but he was already nowhere in sight.

Returning to the house, Maggie used the back stairs to the second floor and climbed the narrow steps into the attic. When she pushed open the door, heat hit her face as if a blanket had fallen from the ceiling. Dust and cobwebs covering one side of the room assured her Jesse had nothing hidden there, but on the other side boxes had been moved and cobwebs cleared away.

In the center of the cleared area lay a worn script of *Hamlet*, scribbled over with notes and hashmarks and some yellow highlighting. In a zippered satchel, Maggie found Jesse's signed contract with the Shakespeare Festival, random receipts, a folded copy of the notice Franny had posted on the bulletin board at McLaughlin College, and most interesting, a packet of letters bound with rubber bands. She took it all with her.

Downstairs once more, she sat down to examine the letters. They were all in one handwriting, mostly in black pen, but the envelopes were missing. She skimmed several letters, then stopped to put them in sequential order before beginning to read again. The letter writer usually signed his first initial—*M*—but the most emotional of the letters, one in which he alluded to suicide, bore his name, Mark.

Maggie could hear the anguish of this on-again, off-again love affair between the two young men. Over the span of four months, Jesse was the love of Mark's life, the center of his universe, the cruelest of betrayers, and the most deceitful man ever born. Jesse had sent Mark a dozen "gorgeous long-stemmed roses" to beg forgiveness for talking to another guy in a bar; Mark had adored them but spent another paragraph mocking "your little Dorothy with the man-bun."

Now the "You'll be sorry" she had found on the torn-up note under Jesse's pillow made more sense. If Mark had gone through with the suicide, someone might be blaming Jesse.

She examined the notice about the documents and found in the upper right a scribbled note: "Jesse, this is the job I was telling you about. There could be a big payoff! Perfect for you." It was unsigned.

Maggie sat thinking a while, then dialed Jimmy Callahan's number.

"Hagan's Crossing *Po*-lice."

"Amanda, this is Maggie O'Malley. I need to talk to Chief Callahan right away."

"He's in the back room. Deputy Kramer is right here, though."

"*No*." Maggie was aware she had almost shouted the word.

"Well, all right." Amanda sounded wounded. "I'll put you on hold and get him."

"Thank you, I'm sorry, Amanda."

In about a minute, the chief picked up. "This is Callahan." Amanda hadn't told him who was calling. He listened silently to Maggie's narrative.

"At least we know he's alive," he said when she was done.

"Yeah, but Jimmy, he looks awful. He's got a big secret, and I think he's in danger."

"Whaddya mean?"

"I found scraps of a torn-up note threatening him—'you'll be sorry'—and in the attic I found a packet of letters from Mark, obviously a boyfriend—a boyfriend who might have committed suicide."

"I'm gonna need all that," Callahan said. "You think the threat is from another boyfriend of Mark's? Was it signed?"

"No, it wasn't."

"I dunno," Callahan said. "Sounds like jealousy to me. I wonder if there was a relationship between Ron and Jesse. I'm gonna question some of the cast members again."

Maggie didn't think Jimmy was on the right track, but she let it go.

Callahan asked Maggie to drop off the papers she had found and said he would send Kramer to Franny's house to check the attic one more time and seal the house again.

"I think you need to change the locks. Jesse has a key," she said.

"Yeah, I'll get Kramer on that too. So it isn't likely he climbed in the kitchen window if he had a key . . ." Callahan said, thinking out loud.

Maggie went back out to her car and sat thinking. Glancing at her side mirror, she was surprised to see that the man in the maroon car had parked on the cross street, facing Woodbine. He hadn't been there earlier.

"He must not know Franny is dead," she thought. "Or it isn't Franny he's watching for."

Starting her car, she drove away from Franny's house and went around the block so she could get a closer look.

Passing the maroon car slowly, she smiled at the driver in case he looked at her, but he didn't. He stared straight ahead. A memory of that night backstage in the park flashed into her mind. The costume piece that hadn't fit—there it was: a Cleveland baseball cap.

This man was backstage—dressed in black—during intermission. *He was there for Jesse that night*, Maggie thought. *And all this time he's been watching for him.*

Maggie stopped a block away, where she could see the maroon car in her rearview mirror. She called Jimmy's cell phone, deciding she didn't have time to go through Amanda.

In a flurry of words, Maggie told the chief what she remembered and explained that this man, who had been watching Franny's house, might have gone after Jesse during the play as well as possibly killing Franny that morning. She urged Jimmy to pick him up right away.

He agreed.

"Stay there and keep an eye on him. Do not approach him, do you understand me? I'm serious. I'll send Kramer."

"Yes, sir. Understood, sir," she replied.

–21–

In the Course of Justice

Maggie waited as she'd been instructed, sitting low in her front seat so the man in the maroon car would not see her. It began to rain, which gave her a little more cover, so she relaxed a little, waiting for Officer Kramer. He arrived within 15 minutes from the direction of downtown and hit his lights with a blast of siren as he pulled in front of the maroon car. It was a quick transaction: he walked to the driver's side and asked for a license, which he scrutinized for a minute. Maggie saw the man get out of the car and stand limply near the trunk. She was too far away to hear, but she knew Kramer had ordered him to put his hands on the car before patting him down, pulling his arms behind him, and cuffing his wrists. The driver looked miserable, with water running off the bill of his baseball cap and soaking into his cotton shirt and pants. Kramer was none too gentle in the way he was handling the man. He, at least, had on a raincoat and a plastic cover on his cap.

Maggie went home, driving slowly because the rain had become torrential, the result of rising June heat and humidity. She was making headway in her search of the trunks, and she planned to spend the afternoon and evening digging to the bottom. Her sadness fueled her resolve to find out what had happened to Franny. There was no proof that her death was anything more than an accident, but its timing made Maggie uneasy. She knew Franny had been frightened by a stranger who had come wanting to see the documents. And then there was this man who parked and watched the house. She thought back to the vision of Franny inviting her into the house and how radiant she had looked. There was some comfort in that.

Kramer returned to the police station in a foul mood since he was soaking wet despite the rain gear—and since he had noticed Maggie O'Malley sitting in her car down the block from where he had picked up the suspect.

"I shoulda known she'd be in the middle of things," he muttered to himself. "That woman doesn't know her place."

He ushered the man, who was also soaking wet, into the station and led him into an interrogation room. It was 10 by 12 feet, windowless, with gunmetal gray walls, a gray painted floor, and a single fluorescent light hanging from the ceiling. In the center of the room was a metal table, bolted to the floor, with two metal chairs on each side.

Kramer led the man to a chair and pushed him down into it, freeing his left hand while cuffing his right hand to a circular extension on the table.

"Could I have a cup of coffee?" the prisoner asked.

Kramer just looked at him and snorted, then left the room.

He went to Chief Callahan's office and described all that had happened, adding the comment that he had seen Maggie

O'Malley with her nose in it. This Jimmy ignored. He took the driver's license Kramer had confiscated and instructed him to type up an initial report.

"Like you told me, I didn't arrest him," Kramer said. "I told him he was being detained as a material witness."

Callahan nodded and went into the interrogation room, pulling another patrolman inside to stand next to the door. He sat down facing the man, who was still soaking wet, and handed him a wad of paper towels.

"Mr. Lindauer, I see. Edward M. Lindauer from Hinckley, Ohio. Where is that exactly?"

"Near Cleveland. I'd like to know why I was arrested."

"You're not under arrest, Mr. Lindauer; you're being detained as a material witness."

"Witness to what?" Lindauer asked.

Callahan ignored the question. "What brought you to Hagan's Crossing?"

"I came looking for a friend."

"And who would that be?"

Lindauer was silent.

"If you haven't done anything wrong, Mr. Lindauer, there's no reason you shouldn't answer my questions."

More silence.

"Well, sir, we have a witness who saw you backstage at the park last Thursday night, when one of the actors died onstage. Another young man—who was supposed to be in that actor's costume—has disappeared, and it seems he comes from your part of Ohio. Now can you explain why you came to Hagan's Crossing and why you've spent so many hours parked on Willow Avenue in sight of a home on Woodbine?"

"How long are you going to hold me?"

"I don't rightly know. Two people have died, Mr. Lindauer. You have been seen in the vicinity of both deaths."

Lindauer was silent.

Callahan waited 30 seconds and then got up to leave, telling the officer by the door, "Get him a cup of coffee and a blanket."

Over the next several hours, Callahan applied for a search warrant for Lindauer's car and acquired his driving record and basic stats from the police in Hinckley. He found out Lindauer was a retired chemist whose only son Mark had died the previous year. The inquest had ruled the death a suicide. There was a memorial Facebook page with condolences from friends and pictures of Mark with Jesse Gilmer.

Wait, that's not right—maybe a typo? Callahan thought. *Or Jesse came here under a false name. Was he running from Lindauer?*

It was getting dark when Callahan went back into the interrogation room. Lindauer raised his head and said, "I thought you were never coming back."

Callahan placed a ham sandwich and bottle of water on the table and sat down opposite Lindauer.

"I understand you had a son, Mark, who died. I'm sorry for your loss." He paused, waiting for a response. Lindauer said nothing. "While you eat that, you can tell me the truth about your pursuit of Jesse Gilemorane and his relationship with Mark."

Lindauer had looked up quizzically at the mention of Jesse's name.

"There is no point in lying to me. I know what you did. You came here to get revenge on Jesse because of your son's death. And Jesse's real name is Gilmer—which you know. You're a chemist. You prepared the vial of cyanide and DMSO that you put into Ron Spear's ear— thinking he was Jesse. Isn't that the truth?"

Lindauer protested. He admitted he had come to find Jesse but denied any involvement in the young actor's death. He challenged the chief to produce any evidence.

"You were watching the house on Woodbine," Callahan said. "Did you enter that house at any time?"

"No."

Callahan pressed him.

"You didn't go into the house searching for Jesse?"

"No—I didn't even approach the house. I just watched because I wanted to talk to Jesse," Lindauer insisted.

Callahan shifted focus.

"What exactly was the relationship between Jesse and Mark?"

"It's none of your damn business," Lindauer shot back.

"Well, it is, because I have a note you wrote to Jesse—a threat you made because of Mark."

"Mark was a good boy. A good boy. Until he started up with that crowd going to those bars on the lake—that Leather Horse or something like that—and he changed—he changed so that I hardly knew him."

Lindauer looked pale and defeated, though this flare of anger put at least some color in his face. Callahan noticed the nervous twitch of the man's left eyelid. *Probably a result of exhaustion*, he thought. He waited for Lindauer to look up from the table.

"You didn't approve of your son being gay?" Callahan asked.

"I just wanted my boy back."

"So does Mrs. Spear."

"I didn't kill him, I swear."

Callahan left the room and called Maggie to ask if Jesse had said anything to her about Mark.

"No, I didn't mention his name—I just asked if he had been threatened. That's what made him jump up in a panic."

"I just feel like Lindauer did it," Jimmy said. "Unless he confesses, though, I don't have enough to charge him. Shit. Plus, there's a reason we can't find graduation or motor vehicle records—Jesse's been using a false name. I found a Facebook page memorializing Mark Lindauer, and pictures of Jesse and Mark are all over it. Jesse's real name is Gilmer."

"That explains no Gilemoranes in the census records. It seems as if he might have been trying to disappear, but Lindauer found him," Maggie said. "I'm sorry I don't have any more information."

Callahan saw that Lindauer was clearly angry with Jesse, had been following him, and had the chemical know-how to have made the poison, but without evidence to charge him with a crime, Callahan grudgingly released him. The search warrant hadn't come through yet either. He advised Lindauer not to leave town. He directed an officer to drive him back to his car on Willow Avenue.

Eddie Lindauer got out of the police car and watched the officer drive away. He was still damp all the way to his skin, and he was hungry, but mostly he was exhausted.

He climbed into the back seat and went to sleep.

–22–

So Foul and Fair a Day

Avery Prendergast was at a loss. He had gotten back to the hotel room in the wee hours of Monday morning and finally fallen dead asleep from exhaustion. Now, in the light of day, he debated how to proceed. He had always considered himself a dealmaker, but now he wondered if he had gotten in out of his depth.

It was late Monday afternoon, and Avery sat surveying the comfortable suite, with its fridge and kitchenette. He decided to stay and wait to hear from the man who had contacted him in Cleveland.

About 2:00 p.m., he walked down the street to the Cup 'n Saucer to get lunch and bring back another sandwich and a drink for later. Customers were discussing the discovery that Franny Babcock had been found dead. A wave of panic hit him. Had anyone seen him at her house? Did anyone know he had been there asking for access to the documents? Did they know how she had died?

He sat for a long while eavesdropping on the gossip, waiting to hear if there were any mention of him or the trunks. The three women and one man sitting at the adjoining table were on a second cup of coffee and in no hurry either. The oldest woman, with slightly blue-tinged hair, took the lead in explaining that Franny had unfortunately let that actor fellow come to live in her back bedroom, and he had disappeared. She said she had gone to school with Franny and knew her to be altogether too trusting of strangers. She always had been that way, and now look what had happened.

The woman seated with her back to Avery, wearing a '60s-style pillbox hat, agreed that something was going on with Franny; she lowered her voice to say that her niece who lived across the street from Franny had seen the handyman and his son carry two big wooden trunks out of her house and drive them away just last Friday. What in the world could have been in those trunks?

The man, who seemed to be with Pillbox—probably her husband, from the tone of his voice—scoffed at the idea of anything mysterious. He said there was no reason to see a connection between the trunks and Franny's death. Pillbox retorted with something that made the group laugh, but Avery didn't catch it. The woman in wire-rimmed glasses, who hadn't spoken yet, interjected that if anyone in town would know what was going on, it would be Maggie O'Malley, who made it her business to find out everybody else's business. Pillbox's husband responded with an "Oh, now," and defended Maggie: "Sure, she's a researcher—of course she finds out information." Pillbox gave him a withering look.

"It's dollars to doughnuts that Maggie has got hold of those papers Franny Babcock was braggin' about finding. That's all I'm saying," she said.

"So how did she die?" asked Wire-Rims. "Did she have a stroke?"

"Or did someone strike her?" asked Blue Hair. She seemed

to take a ghoulish delight in the remark, Avery thought, and she followed it up with an observation that the police chief might be overwhelmed by two unexplained deaths in one week. Wire-Rims said what Callahan ought to be concerned by was the number of strangers who'd come to town recently.

By this time, Avery had finished his pie, drained the third cup of coffee, and received his to- go order. The last remark signaled he shouldn't hang around anymore. Blue Hair had already given him a couple of quizzical looks, and he thought she had darted her eyes toward him as if to say to Pillbox, "Take a look at what's behind you."

Walking back to the hotel, he wondered if the conversation had shifted to him after he left. *Stop being paranoid, Ave, ole buddy*, he thought. A three-block walk in the humidity had beaded his forehead with sweat by the time he reached his room. He collapsed on the bed and turned on the television.

He must have fallen asleep briefly, because he was jolted awake by a siren passing by. What he wouldn't give now for a bottle of whiskey. Maybe it wasn't safe to go out again, and besides, he would have to ask directions to a liquor store. That guy had promised to meet him Thursday night, but then the play was stopped halfway through, and he didn't show. He just vanished. Avery wished he knew what the hell was going on.

The phone in the room rang, and Avery answered with hesitation. A man's voice, somewhat muffled, asked, "Mr. Prendergast?"

"Yes, this is he."

"I'm sorry I couldn't meet you the other night. It's good that you stayed in town. I hope you've been expecting my call," the man said.

"Yeah, I've been wondering what happened to you," Avery said.

"The other night—things—" He paused. "Things got out of control. I had to handle an unexpected situation."

The voice had an edge to it that made Avery uneasy.

"Yeah, well, that death onstage was very upsetting," Avery said.

There was another pause. Avery wondered if the call had dropped, but then the man quietly said, "Sometimes people die."

Cold, Avery thought. *Oh shit, this guy's crazy.*

"How was your visit to Woodbine Street? Successful?" the man asked.

"No," Avery said. "It wasn't."

"That's very disappointing, Avery. May I call you Avery? I'm deeply disappointed," the voice said.

"I did my best," Avery said.

"Did you?" the voice said. "It's a shame when your best isn't good enough."

Avery felt he was being threatened, but then the speaker brightened his tone.

"No matter. We can still do some business. I have something you will be interested in, and I'm wondering if we could meet."

Avery's mind was racing. What would be the safest thing to do?

"What is it?" he hedged.

"A 19th-century manuscript—from an English poet. I don't want to say any more."

"Do you want to come here?"

"No. If you drive to River Road and go north about three

miles, there's a gravel road that turns off to the right. It leads into some pine trees, and there's a small cabin there. I'll meet you. Wednesday at noon. Bring cash—$300."

The line went dead. Avery called the front desk to see if there was any caller ID. No luck. So, what to do? Should he follow through? Or could this be a trap? It made him nervous to have to hang around another day. He thought again about going out for whiskey, but a late afternoon thunderstorm had popped up, pelting the road and vehicles outside with hail that bounced like ping-pong balls. He would stay put tonight and decide in the morning whether or not to meet the man.

–23–

The Whirligig of Time

It was Monday night, and Maggie was still feeling the shock of finding Franny. She had been sitting and thinking, turning everything over and over in her mind. The grandfather clock struck 9:00, and as Maggie got up to turn the lights on, the doorbell rang.

Through the sidelight, she could see it was Mary Lou.

"Well, isn't this a welcome surprise!" she said brightly, but then she saw that Mary Lou had been crying. Maggie reached out to hug her.

"Oh, Mary Lou, what is it? What's the matter? Come in, come sit down," she said, guiding her friend to the couch.

Mary Lou was wiping her eyes with her palms, so Maggie handed her a tissue.

"I'm sorry, Maggie—I heard about Miss Babcock, and I know you've had a terrible day, but I found something I have to show you."

"It's okay, I'm glad you came; tell me about it," Maggie said. "But first, can I get you something to drink?"

"No, thanks, I'm fine."

She sat still and took a deep breath.

"You know, our visit to Marshall's really started me

thinking and remembering about my grandmother and the stories she told us," Mary Lou said. "So I went searching."

Reaching into the bag she had brought, Mary Lou lifted out a folded piece of quilted patchwork about 36 inches square. It was faded and thin, the batting flattened by storage. The pattern included triangles of perhaps six different patterned fabrics in blue, red, gray, and green, as if it were made from the remnants of calico shirts or dresses. Framing the triangles were larger squares on all four sides.

She handed the quilt to Maggie, saying, "This has been hidden at the bottom of my grandmother's chifforobe for more than 100 years. I had never gone through all her things until now. I had forgotten they were there."

"Oh, this is amazing," Maggie said.

Spreading the square out on the couch between them, both women touched the stitching reverently with their fingertips.

Mary Lou explained that after she had discovered the quilt square in her grandmother's things, she'd found another surprise. Unfolding the fabric, she had felt something crinkly inside a corner square. Trying not to damage the heirloom, she had slit one edge open and pulled out two pieces of folded paper, one a note on tissue in faded writing, the other a torn document.

"You're not going to believe this, Maggie," she said as she unfolded the tissue and spread it on the coffee table. "It was written by Cassie—and I think it has been inside this quilt piece since the 1870s!"

Mary Lou began to read:

God, help me. I don't know what to do, and I am sore afraid to say anything. Maybe it is too dangerous for me to write this, but I want to put the truth down somewhere. The other night I seen Mister Elijah strike and kill my Joseph. Joseph had gone to see what the commotion was in the downstairs office of Mr. Philip, and he tole me to stay put but I followed. I was hid by the door when Joseph surprised Mr. Elijah. Oh Lord, Mr. Elijah was stealing papers from the desk, and Joseph done grabbed at a big one in his hand and it tore in the scuffle. I saw Mr. Elijah raise the lamp and knock Joseph down dead. He picked up one part of the torn paper. Then he was cursing and yelling to the other white men with him, "Find that other piece! I want that paper!" But then the dogs outside began to bark, and the men ran away. I run upstairs and through the house to see them heading for the river. Then I got in my bed under the covers. I'm ashamed I didn't go back to help Joseph. I wondered if I should run away, maybe go to Mister Philip's lawyer in town. But I know that Mr. Elijah would kill me soon as look at me, and if I ran, he coulda said I done it. At daylight, I went downstairs and found Joseph with his head smashed in—I lifted him onto my lap, holding his head, and cried hard, telling him "I'm sorry, I'm sorry, I'm sorry" 'till I couldn't breathe no more. Underneath his body, I found the torn paper Joseph had grabbed from Mr. Elijah. I saw that it was mighty valuable, so I kept it. If Mr. Elijah comes after me, maybe I can use it. After I hid the paper, I screamed and woke the house. Mr. Elijah and the cook come. Then the constables come and Mr. Elijah told a black lie that he was asleep all night. After the constables went away,

I seen Mr. Elijah with a torn paper he took out of his shirt, and when he saw me he looked hate at me 'till the hair stood up on my arms. I am so scared of him. Miss Emma and Mr. Philip have come home and she cried about the papers that was her daddy's and her uncle's. She was at least happy not all the poems was took. I darsant tell anyone what I saw and did. And I pray Joseph forgives me for leaving him to die.

Mary Lou kept her composure until the last two lines, when she began to cry again. Maggie laid the quilt aside and took Mary Lou in her arms for a minute, then handed her another tissue.

"You found this today?" Maggie asked.

"Yeah, and that's not all." Mary Lou unfolded the other piece of paper, the one with the ragged left edge, and handed it to Maggie. "Look at this."

Maggie took the paper carefully.

"What in the world? This is addressed to someone's Aunt Emma."

"Keep reading," Mary Lou said.

Maggie went on, noticing that the document—20 handwritten lines—was missing the opening letters of many. The paper bore the second half of a signature—which Maggie recognized with a shock.

"Oh my God, Mary Lou. This is it. This is the treasure—or half of it. I think somebody has the other half," Maggie said. "And I might know who it is."

"My grandma told us there might not be a treasure, but if there was one, we better learn to read or we'd never know it if we saw it."

"What made you look for this?" Maggie asked.

"This morning I just got to thinking about the chifforobe in the back corner of the basement, and I started wondering if anything was still packed away down there. Grandma Izzy had prized that chifforobe and said Mama needed to keep it. It was so big and scratched up that we put it downstairs. I don't think anyone ever looked in it before—it's just been part of the past, an old piece of furniture it wasn't worth using or giving away."

"Did you find anything else in there?" Maggie said.

"Just a bunch of old sewing patterns, mostly unprinted tissue paper that had been used over and over. There was one really old Butterick envelope for a housedress. The quilt was underneath." Pointing to the note, Mary Lou said, "I think that was written on a piece of a sewing pattern and kept in a place no one would look. Poor Cassie, she must have been so terrified."

"I think I know what happened, Mary Lou, but I want to compare these details with some things in my notes. Can I keep the papers and the quilt for a while?"

"Of course, Mags," Mary Lou said. "I'm so sorry about Miss Babcock. Give me a call if there's anything I can do."

Maggie shut the door and turned to the cats, who had jumped on the couch to investigate the new smells from the quilt.

"Tomorrow," Maggie announced, "I'm going to Farmington."

24

Nature's Infinite Book of Secrets

Tuesday morning Maggie woke up at seven, despite having pored over the documents and researched on the computer until 2:00 a.m. She made some coffee, fed the cats, took her cup into the study, surveyed her discoveries—and looked again at the treasure Mary Lou had found.

She organized the Farmington records, receipts for hemp and other produce sales from the early to mid-1830s, bearing the signature of John Speed, and multiple documents mentioning his children. There were two letters concerning Speed's son Philip and his marriage to Emma Keats, and there were business documents from the estate of Emma's father George.

One of George's first business ventures in Louisville was to invest in a sawmill which became the Smith and Keats Lumber Mill on the north side of Main Street between First and Brook Streets. From a letter, Maggie gleaned that George had lived on a high bank overlooking the Falls of the Ohio while he was still building his fortune. She filled in some details with internet research. George had used profits from the lumber mill to build a grist mill, producing flour, and by

1835 he had built a palatial home on Walnut Street with six bedrooms and a library of 400 volumes. The Keats family became prominent because of his wealth but also because of his brother John's reputation as a poet. Maggie was excited to find an online published review of an edition of Keats's poetry edited by George's grandson, John Gilmer Speed, and a letter from Speed describing his mother's collection of poems and letters written in his great-uncle's own handwriting.

Refilling her coffee, she went back to work in the trunks.

"Oh, this can't be!" Maggie said as she peered closely at a yellowed piece of stationery. It seemed to be the last page of a letter written in a round penmanship, widely spaced. At the bottom of the page she found the signature "Oscar Wilde" and below that, "21 March 1882, Omaha, Nebraska."

"Oscar Wilde! Oh, but where's the beginning of the letter?" she said. "Who's he writing this to?" She flipped through the rest of the stack but didn't find any similar stationery. With excitement, she read aloud to herself:

> *What you have given me is more golden than gold, more precious than any treasure this great country could yield me, though the land be a network of railways and each city a harbor for the galleys of the world.*
>
> *It is a sonnet I have always loved, and indeed who but the supreme and perfect artist could have got from a mere colour a motive so full of marvel; and now I am half enamoured of the paper that touched his hand, and the ink that did his bidding, grown fond of the sweet comeliness of his charactery, for since my boyhood I have loved none better than your marvelous kinsman, that god-like*

boy, the real Adonis of our age, who knew the silver-footed messages of the moon and the secret of the morning, who heard in Hyperion's vale the largest utterance of the early gods and from the beechen plot the light-winged Dryad, who saw Madeline at the painted window and Lamia in the house at Corinth and Endymion ankle deep in lilies of the vale—

Well, she thought, *this is certainly a reference to John Keats.*

A quick internet search revealed that Oscar Wilde had made an 1882 lecture tour of America and that the Louisville event was attended by George Keats's daughter, Emma Keats Speed, then 59 years old. She had sent the original manuscript of "Sonnet on Blue" to Wilde after inviting him to her home to see her uncle's manuscripts.

Wilde had later written, "I spent most of the next day with her, reading the letters of Keats to her father, some of which were at that time unpublished, poring over torn yellow leaves and faded scraps of paper."

No sooner had Maggie read this description than she picked up several faded handwritten pages. The first two pages were sonnets, and at the bottom of the second page was the closing of a letter in which the poems had been transcribed:

—everything is in delightful forwardness; the violets are not withered, before the peeping of the first rose; You must let me know everything, how parcels go and come, what papers you have, and what Newspapers

you want, and other things. God bless you my dear Brother and Sister

Your ever Affectionate Brother
John Keats—

With a catch in her throat, Maggie realized that these pages were written by John Keats to his brother and sister-in-law and that she was holding original poems. Keats had died in 1821, so these pages were more than 200 years old.

"Oh my lord, Franny, Franny—this would have made you so happy." She couldn't stop the tears stinging her eyes.

For ten minutes she sat reading and rereading the fragile papers. Then she lifted several sheets of acid-free paper from a cabinet and carefully tucked the Keats manuscript and the letter from Oscar Wilde inside, putting the packet in a locked desk drawer.

"Emma," she said aloud. "Let's see, when did Emma marry Philip Speed?" Finn had moseyed into the room, and Maggie addressed the question to him. He didn't respond but jumped up onto one of the chests. Maggie had to keep them closed so that the cats wouldn't take up residence. From his vantage point, he watched her every move.

"You're probably here to remind me to feed you, but I don't see why you can't be helpful and answer some of my questions, Finn."

He purred in response to her voice, one of his most endearing qualities, she thought.

She found her notes on key people and dates and saw that Philip and Emma were married in June of 1841, when Emma was only 17.

"And when did George Keats die, Finn?"

Finn curled up on some of the papers.

"You know you're not transparent, cat. Why must you sit exactly where I am trying to read?"

He squeezed his eyes at her and yawned to express his absolute lack of concern.

"Here it is—George died on Christmas Eve, 1841—oh, that's sad. Only six months after Emma's marriage."

Gathering up the documents and notes except for those beneath her feline paperweight— which she determined were not of consequence—Maggie decided to make the visit she had planned to Farmington. While she was dressing, her thoughts turned over and over the puzzle of Jesse's involvement in the documents.

Although she could get to Louisville more quickly by interstate, she decided she would take River Road, which wound its way to the city at a more leisurely pace. It didn't take her long to make a tuna sandwich, grab an apple, and fill a bottle of water for the road. She slipped on jeans and a University of Louisville T-shirt Danny had given her. He was a dedicated Cardinals fan. "When in Rome," she said aloud.

Walking out to the Prius, Maggie felt buoyed by the sunshine and her sense of anticipation. Her mood sank briefly, however, when she had some difficulty starting the car. She pushed the starter button and . . . nothing. She sat for a minute, taking deep breaths—as if her being calm were important to the car. This idea amused her. Never let a machine know you are upset! She tried a second time and the engine started. Crisis averted.

"I guess I need to get the battery looked at," she said aloud.

The late-morning sun sprinkled light on the road through the canopy of cottonwoods and water maples that lined the river. A breeze coming off the water on her right rippled through the leaves, making them nod like bobbleheads. Each leaf became a face and each tree a crowd engaged in lively conversation. She imagined the stately trees, some conversing with the wind, some musing among themselves with some prescience about the occasionally passing motorists. Where the shade grew deepest along the road, Maggie imagined the trees became philosophical.

"That one wants to know what we know."

"Yes, but how could she? Our roots lie deep beneath this riverbed. Long ago they pierced the wooden coffins buried here and twined themselves around the bones of the forgotten dead."

"These humans cannot draw from the well of memory as we can. They can never know what we know. They build roads and fly past in their cars and have no idea what the trees and the river know."

"True. They cannot even see what the eagle sees from her nest in my tallest branches."

Then, as if a spell were broken, Maggie shook her head and said aloud, "Geez, where did that come from?" The road opened into a clearing and the voices of the whispering trees faded away. The sunlight glistening on the river lifted the mood, and Maggie realized she was nearly at the point of entering the city. She found the almost-hidden spot on Bardstown Road near a busy intersecting highway where a small sign with an arrow pointed the way down a residential street: "To Farmington."

Quickly, however, the street turned into a narrow, one-way lane overhung with green, as if in one moment she were driving through a modern subdivision and in the next she were tunneling into the past. The drive opened into a parking lot in front of a long, squat visitors' center with a wide porch and multiple wooden rocking chairs. Inside she was greeted by a docent who welcomed her with the news that the next tour would begin in 15 minutes and that she could either look at the photos on display inside or walk around the grounds.

Happy to explore outside, Maggie crossed a stone bridge over a stream that had once been much larger and the primary water source for the plantation. Straddling the creek was a springhouse built of limestone. She read the posted explanation that it was the 1820s equivalent of refrigeration; ice cut from the frozen stream in winter could last in the springhouse as late as April or May.

Next to the stone bridge, Maggie entered a small, square memorial area lined with stone benches, dedicated "in the memory of the enslaved African Americans" who had built and worked at Farmington under the ownership of the Speeds. She sat, closed her eyes and spoke to Athena and Cassie: "I am so sorry for the pain you endured. I hope you can see my friend Mary Lou, what a good, strong woman she has become."

> *She opened her eyes to catch sight of a young Black woman at least 50 yards away, wearing a long cotton dress, her head tied in a bandanna. The woman gazed at Maggie for a full 30 seconds, then turned away and was gone.*

"Thank you," Maggie whispered. It was another five minutes before she felt composed enough to move on.

Returning to the visitors' center, Maggie joined three others in watching an audiovisual presentation on the significance of Farmington, not only as a large working plantation in pre- Civil-War Kentucky but also as a site associated with Abraham Lincoln. Lincoln's friendship with Joshua Fry Speed had begun when both young men lived in Springfield, Illinois. Speed had opened a dry goods store and Lincoln was a struggling lawyer.

Although both Kentuckians, they were unknown to each other until Speed agreed to share his lodgings above the store with a destitute Lincoln—and the result was a lifelong friendship. Maggie learned that Joshua Speed had reluctantly returned to Farmington to help settle the estate after his father's death in March of 1840, leaving Lincoln in Springfield. By the beginning of the next year, Lincoln's melancholy temperament had flared into a dangerous depression, attributed to his troubled relationship with Mary Todd. Apparently, Lincoln's friends were truly worried he would harm himself. In the spring, Joshua Speed invited Lincoln to come to Farmington as a respite, an invitation Lincoln accepted in the summer of 1841.

When the docent led the visitors up the front steps of the Federal-style brick home, she stopped on the porch to describe the arrival and departure of Lincoln from the house. "He stood right here," she said, directing her words to a nine-year-old boy. "The 16th president of the United States touched this doorknob and stood on this porch." The child might not have felt much awe, but Maggie did—a feeling that grew as the tour continued and the docent focused more and more on the history of Lincoln's visit.

As they gathered in the dining room, looking at the table set with Lucy Fry Speed's original china, the docent stood behind the chair Lincoln had occupied and related the story of a dinner party at which the untutored Lincoln, lacking social graces, neglected to pass the dishes properly, shocking the other guests. He had enjoyed Lucy Speed's peaches and cream enormously. He had been wrapped in the affection of Joshua's mother, sisters, and sister-in-law.

Throughout the 14-room house, upstairs and down, the docent made connections between life at Farmington and Lincoln's visit during August and September 1841. In the sitting room, Maggie stood for a long while looking at the portraits of the Speeds' grown children, particularly Joshua, who had been Lincoln's friend, and Philip, who had brought his 17-year-old wife Emma to live at Farmington during the summer of 1841.

In fact, the docent pointed out, Lincoln took something of Farmington with him. Apparently, the visit did lift Lincoln from that bout of melancholy, and it inspired him to embrace a higher purpose. When he left, Lucy Speed gave him an Oxford Bible with the advice that it would be the greatest antidote to his depression. The docent pointed out a framed thank-you letter Lincoln had sent to Mary, the Speeds' oldest daughter: "Tell your mother that I have not got her 'present' [an 'Oxford' Bible] with me, but I intend to read it regularly when I return home. I doubt not that it is really, as she says, the best cure for the blues, could one but take it according to the truth. Give my respects to all your sisters (including 'Aunt Emma')."

"Oh." Maggie drew in a sharp breath. "Aunt Emma."

The pieces began falling into place.

The docent, standing near her, said, "What, dear?"

The question didn't resonate at first, as Maggie was lost

in her thoughts. Seconds later, she heard the words and replied, "Oh, I'm sorry, nothing. It's just so interesting."

She determined to examine every single document in those trunks as soon as possible.

On the way home, she thought of Franny and Jesse and the oddness of their coming together. Who in town had contacted Jesse?

25

It Is the Stars, the Stars above Us

No one in Hagan's Crossing knew that Franny Babcock had had a niece, the daughter of her late brother. Ellen Elizabeth Babcock had never been to Hagan's Crossing and didn't even recall having met her Aunt Franny. She was, after all, only two years old when Franny visited her family in Philadelphia. Ellen was stunned to receive an email from Franny's attorney, Hank Watterson, informing her of her aunt's death.

While Hagan's Crossing was speculating about what would happen to Franny's house and property—indeed, what would happen to Franny's remains—Ellen found herself making arrangements to fly to Louisville, rent a car, drive to Hagan's Crossing, and attend a funeral. The attorney assured Ellen by phone that Franny had preplanned and paid for most of the arrangements: she had chosen the funeral parlor, selected a headstone, and even written her own obituary to be placed in the *Clarion*. She had left minimal decisions to be made, mostly regarding flowers and food for a reception.

"Would you like me to contact the funeral parlor for you, Ms. Babcock, to schedule the calling?" Mr. Watterson asked.

"Uh, well, I suppose so. Is a calling the same as a visitation?"

"Yes. The calling hours will be inserted into the obituary, and you can expect that most of the town will attend. Your aunt was very well known. Besides, in a small town with southern leanings, a funeral is a very important event."

"I'm afraid I don't know what to do. Did my aunt have any close friends who might advise me on some of the details?"

"I suppose Maggie O'Malley might be someone you could talk with. In fact, just last Friday your aunt stopped in my office to add a codicil to her will saying that two trunks of old documents she had given to Ms. O'Malley were to be listed as a formal bequest. I can give you Ms. O'Malley's phone number and some other details in an email. From the way your aunt spoke of her, I assume they were close friends, although Maggie is quite a bit younger. You and I will also have to schedule a reading of the will, which by tradition takes place following the funeral and committal."

"Committal?"

"The burial. Miss Babcock has requested a graveside service following the funeral."

"Thank you, Mr. Watterson. I appreciate your help," Ellen said. "You know, I had completely forgotten about my aunt—and I feel a little guilty receiving any kind of inheritance."

"Miss Babcock told me you were her only living relative; she had no children or surviving siblings."

"Yes. My father was her only brother, and I'm an only child."

"I wonder that you never got to know Miss Babcock," he said.

"Well, I was raised by an aunt on my mother's side after my parents died together in a car crash when I was five."

"Oh, pardon me, I'm so sorry," he said. He felt embarrassed. "You can rest assured, Ms. Babcock, that the people of Hagan's Crossing will welcome you graciously. I'll send you the additional information you need right away."

Hanging up the phone, Ellen did an internet search for the property valuation office in Oldham County, Kentucky. When she entered her aunt's address and the image of the large Victorian house appeared on the screen, she drew in a breath.

"Hel . . . lo, Aunt Franny," she said aloud, drawing out the words in a tone of surprise. "What a beautiful house!" Under the photo, the assessed value of the property seemed unreal. She gave an audible gasp. It looked as if she had inherited a chunk of the 19th century!

Ellen called the funeral home and scheduled the visitation for the next Friday, with the burial on Saturday. The mortician tried to persuade her that so many people attending would warrant two days of visitation, but she imagined the horror of being consoled for three days by hundreds of strangers for a loss she didn't really feel, and she insisted on one day, from 3:00–5:00 and 6:00–8:30 p.m. He agreed with her aunt's lawyer that Maggie O'Malley would be an ideal contact to help her with arrangements, and he assured Ellen that he would place the obituary immediately online and in the *Clarion*.

And so, on her way home from Farmington, Maggie got a surprising call from Ellen Babcock, explaining that she was

Franny's niece and would be coming to Hagan's Crossing for the funeral. Ellen sounded young and inexperienced; her parents were deceased, and she said she had only attended one funeral in her life; certainly she had never planned one. Maggie agreed to help arrange food and a gathering for after the burial, and Ellen's relief was audible.

Their conversation became awkward, however, when Ellen asked how her aunt had died. "Her attorney only told me she had passed away unexpectedly, and I know she was in her late 80s. What happened?"

Maggie decided not to go into the possibility of murder, so she said that Franny had fallen on the stairs; a terrible accident, as far as she knew. Ellen expressed her surprise and her feeling of guilt at not having known her aunt, and Maggie consoled her, saying that Franny was a strong woman who knew her own mind.

Maggie was about to slip into the house through the sunroom, but before she could reach the door, Jimmy Callahan's secretary, Amanda Filcher, yoo-hooed from the back fence that separated their yards. Maggie always dreaded being caught by Amanda, who had recently added genealogy to her list of obsessions. Amanda's disregard for punctuation—or even full sentences—made conversation difficult. And after almost yelling at Amanda the day before on the phone, Maggie didn't know what to expect.

"Oh, Maggie, I wanted to talk to you." Amanda lowered her voice as though she might be overheard and adopted a conspiratorial tone. "There just might be a stalker in Hagan's Crossing and I think you ought to be careful coming and going because you know I heard Cal talking on the phone to someone about a suspicious car I think is red. I don't think he said 'scarlet,'

I— oh—that's it—maroon—he said there's a maroon car being driven by a man with dark glasses us single ladies have to stick together—so you ought to know. I haven't seen the car myself but believe you me from now on I'm gonna watch for it, because Officer Kramer picked him up, but the Chief had to let him go and for heaven's sake, with that young man murdered in the park and the one who I guess was supposed to be killed missing—you don't know if we're safe or not. It used to be you knew everybody in town and now it's strangers coming in and getting themselves murdered. I mean not everyone because Franny Babcock wasn't from out of town, but her falling down the stairs is pretty suspicious. The chief is fit to be tied over that Jesse fella. I think the chief ought to contact Homeland Security but of course I can't tell him that. Like I said, we have to look out for each other and I'm thinking if they even start that play up again in the park, who knows if it will be safe to go?"

Amanda finally took a breath, and Maggie assured her that the park would definitely be safe when the play opened again.

"Or, you know," Amanda went on, "there might be a serial killer. Oh, and I meant to tell you I found the most alarming piece of information about my grandfather when I called up to the library in Cincinnati that's Hamilton County Ohio in the reference room a woman told me she found his obituary in something called microfiche—isn't that a funny name like little fish swimming around with newspaper articles!" She laughed a high-pitched giggle. "My grandfather died when his house was broken into that sent chills through me considering all this and hearing about Franny. Also, look at this"—she pointed to the ground—"somebody's been tramping through my lettuce, although it's getting hot and it's about to go to seed."

"Amanda, that culprit is probably the rabbit who lives under your back deck. Finn and Fiona watch him from the back of the sunroom couch and chatter like squirrels at him. Then they complain bitterly to me about having to be indoor cats."

Amanda laughed again, and Maggie said she needed to get inside to feed her little predators, so they parted. Once inside, Maggie looked back to see Amanda bent over her lettuce plants, trying to prop them up.

She phoned Mary Lou to arrange a catered lunch after Franny's funeral on Saturday, reserved the hall at the Episcopal church, and sat down to make notes about Farmington and the Speeds.

"This is getting interesting, Finn," she said to the lounging cat. He purred in response to her voice, and she smiled. "Oh, look at the time, cat—Danny's picking me up in half an hour!"

—26—

The Acting of a Dreadful Thing

1874, ENDYMION PLANTATION, KENTUCKY

The rowboat carrying the three men pushed off from the Kentucky side of the river, a mile north of Louisville, just after 9:00 p.m. They had chosen a moonless night, and the dim rays of the small lantern at the bow were cast onto the water and reflected back from the rising mists, creating the eerie illusion of figures moving past.

"If this ain't the worst night you could have picked for this," one of the younger man snarled to the older man who sat in front. "I'm froze already, and we cain't see fer nothin'."

"Shut yer mouth, Jack, and row," said the older man, Mangan, whose authority was established by his having a long pole to steer them away from the riverbank, his control of the lantern, and his possession of a pistol tucked into a holster at his side.

The third man, Jed, bundled up like the others in a thick denim jacket, said nothing but pulled hard on the oar to move the boat upriver.

"At least the wind ain't blowin' in our faces," Mangan

said. "Stay as near the bank as you can. We don't know what barges might be coming down the river, and this fog ain't gonna lift anytime soon."

Lying in the bottom of the boat were several crowbars, a chisel, a hammer, and burlap bags, tools of the men's trade.

For the next seven hours, as the two young men rowed and cursed the cold, the older man meted out swigs of brandy from a leather bottle and kept reminding them of the wealth they would soon have.

"This place is a fine plantation house, I tell you, high on a bluff overlookin' the river, and there's jewels and cash and thousands in bonds for the takin'. Jest remember we have to lay low for a while, but the caretaker swears there's a fortune to be had."

Along about 2:00 a.m. they saw an enormous black barge, at least 150 feet wide, bearing down on them from out of the fog. Loaded down with coal, it looked like some biblical leviathan rising up from the black water. Mangan raised the alarm. "Move, move, get to shore! We'll be hit or knocked over by the wake. You fools drifted too far toward the center." His yelling attracted the attention of a bargeman who rang a large bell hanging from a post on the port side. Moving as close as they could to the Kentucky bank, the men in the rowboat held as still as possible until three long barges pushed by a steam tugboat had passed.

"Damn. That was bad. We've lost a lot of time—and we've been seen by somebody," said Jack.

"He'll be in New Orleans before anybody knows what happened; he ain't no threat to us," Mangan snarled. "But you're right about the time. Pull out into the stream and pull them oars faster, boys."

Finally, a little past 4:30 a.m., they rounded a bend in the river and saw the three-story house, a single light gleaming from a high window. Mangan gave a low whistle. "There 'tis—row her to the shore now," he commanded. Giving Jack a shove, he said, "Jed, get up on the bank and pull her in."

Jed jumped rather than slipped into the water, creating a splash.

"Damn it all, man," Jack hissed, "be quiet."

All three got out of the boat to pull it onto a shelf of limestone shielded by overhanging cottonwood branches. Taking the tools and burlap bags, they began to scale the steep hillside, following Mangan's lantern, which swung and bobbed like a giant firefly in the brush.

They reached the top. From the grove of trees, they could see the outline of the house shrouded in darkness. Mangan made another low whistle and waited. He whistled again and heard an answering call like an owl. A light appeared on the first floor in the center of the house and a window was raised slowly by an unseen hand. A second call came from the house, and Mangan motioned the others to follow him. Crouching low, they ran to the open window; raising it fully, Mangan passed the lantern to Jack and climbed in; then, taking it back again, he motioned the other two to follow him.

The caretaker, a stocky, stubble-faced man, stood in the hallway to lead them through the house. They first stopped in the dining room, where they filled a burlap bag with silver bowls, candlesticks, and goblets. Jack flinched when Jed dropped a handful of silver into the bag with a clatter.

"Ain't nobody home, is there?" Mangan asked the caregiver.

"They all gone 'cept the Negro servants, but they're dead asleep on t'other side of the house," he answered.

Relieved, the younger men filled the bag full.

"Leave it—we'll take it on the way out," Mangan ordered. Then they followed the caretaker to a stairway and down to an office fitted out on the bottom floor. There were two small desks and one large one as well as a sizable iron safe. The caretaker lit a lamp on the desk and handed Mangan several more burlap bags.

Setting to work with the chisels and hammers, they pried open the drawers of the large desk, finding stacks of papers that they swept into bags. Same with the smaller desks; they took everything: pens, letter openers, a small gold watch, even blank folio paper—anything they could sell. Using a large crowbar, they began on the safe, using such force that the door came off its hinges, making a ringing crash as it fell.

The caretaker cursed. "Why didn't you jest bring a church bell with you, you damn fools?"

From the shelves of the safe they pulled stacks of banknotes and bonds, bundles of old documents tied up in ribbon, and loose papers with faded handwriting.

"How do we know this here is worth takin'?" Jack asked. "It's a damn lot to carry."

"It's been kept in a safe, you idiot; it must be worth something. Shut up and keep workin'," Mangan growled.

A loud voice hollered out from the hallway.

"What's goin' on in there? Who is that?"

An elderly Black man appeared in the doorway, holding a large candlestick and candle above his head. The burglars froze, watching to see what would happen next.

Looking at the caretaker, the old man said, "Why, suh, what you doin' in here? You men are robbin' the place? Lord, no, that ain't right."

"Damn, Joseph, this ain't none of your business," the caretaker snarled. He had been examining a large document, and he swung around as he spoke, holding the paper in front of him. Joseph swung the candlestick at the caretaker but missed his mark. He only succeeded in snuffing out the flame. At the same time—with his other hand—he snatched at the paper, which tore almost down the middle. Picking up the oil lamp, the caretaker smashed it into Joseph's head, knocking him down, extinguishing the light. Unwittingly, he dropped his half of the torn paper back into the mess on the floor. He yelled for the others to find the paper he had dropped, but they stood in shock. The caretaker spotted it and picked it up, slipping it into an inside pocket.

Then they stood for a long moment over Joseph's still body.

"We didn't 'spect to kill nobody," Jack said at last.

"Shut up," Mangan said. "Somebody relight that lamp or fetch another." He turned to the caretaker. "Who else is here? Who's gonna come in here next in response to this commotion?"

"Mebbe his wife or the cook," the caretaker said.

"Darn it all. This is a peck o' trouble," Mangan muttered.

"What about the jewels?" Jed asked. "Ain't we gonna find them now?"

"T'aint safe to stay longer. Joseph's woman might have woke up too. You fellas gotta go." The caretaker barked these orders at Mangan, who directed the younger men to gather up the bags containing cash, bonds, and large amounts of personal papers. They left piles of paper strewn around. The caretaker urged them back up the stairs, opened the front door, and told them to run for it.

"What about the silver?"

"No time. Jest *go*," he hissed at them.

He watched until they disappeared into the woods, then went back downstairs to the office. He stood over the body of the old Black man, looking at his caved-in skull. *Good riddance*, he thought. Picking up a crowbar, he went outside and around to the dining room window, shut it, and pried at it in several places, being sure to chip off some wood in the process.

Remembering the torn document, he returned to the basement to search. What about the other half? He bent down, rifling through the pile, but footsteps on the floor above meant he had to get back to his quarters. He didn't want to be found here. He'd find it later, he thought.

Hours later, when the sun rose, a woman screaming roused him from sleep.

–27–

Give Sorrow Words

While she dressed, Maggie went over her last conversation with Danny. He had said "I love you" and she had answered "I love you too." She wondered if her response had been too mechanical. She thought Danny's feelings for her were stronger than hers for him. She didn't want to lose her independence, but she didn't want him to lose interest. She enjoyed his company and, to some extent, his protective attitude. He was an attractive man, his hair once black and now salt-and-pepper gray, and his brown eyes held her warmly in his gaze. She thought of his smile, the cut of his jaw, the features that made him so sexy, but then she stopped herself.

"You don't have time for this, Maggie," she said aloud. "Romance is for later."

She thought how glad she was that she had cut her hair shorter for the summer months, even though Danny wanted her to wear it longer. She liked it just above her earlobes and styled in a bob that was easy to blow-dry.

"What is it with men and long hair?" She addressed this question to Fiona, who had sauntered into the bedroom. Fiona responded by collapsing onto Maggie's white sandals.

The evening was bound to be warm, but there was always a breeze from the river, so Maggie selected a flowered cotton sundress in blue and green with a bolero jacket. The flowers reminded her of Franny's blue hydrangeas, and she felt a little guilty dressing to go out to dinner—she hated to think of Franny's body in a morgue.

Here I am going on a date, and for Franny, life's . . . over. This thought was followed by another wave of anger. If only she knew where to aim it!

Danny was prompt as always, and Maggie was a little surprised at how glad she was to see his warm smile through the screen door. Then she surprised both herself and him by bursting into tears.

"Mags, oh, honey?" He opened the screen, and she stepped into his arms. Finally it felt safe to let go, and Maggie's body relaxed against Danny's; she sobbed until she had exhausted herself. He continued to hold her, stroking her back, and then guided her to the sofa, where he pulled her close. Finally her crying slowed to a kind of moan, then to a silent gasping for air, as if her lungs could not relinquish her sadness.

He handed her a clean handkerchief.

"I'm sorry, Danny, I've got"—she blew her nose—"snot and tears all over your shirt. And now I'm a mess, and this is a mess," she said, holding up the handkerchief smeared with mascara and eye shadow.

"That doesn't matter," he said. "Talk to me."

The comment nearly triggered her tears again, but she took a deep breath and told him about the events of the previous morning: finding Franny with her head bloodied, Cecil trying to get to his feet. She described how the medical examiners had processed the scene and taken Franny's body away. More hesitantly, she told him about her discovery of Jesse and how he'd gotten away again.

"Mags, you could have been in danger, going back into the house with him! You called Jimmy, didn't you? You can't judge by how clean-cut and charming someone is. Ted Bundy looked and acted like an Eagle Scout, and he killed at least 30 women! Promise me you'll be careful."

"I will. I promise. But I'd really like to go to dinner now; I've hardly eaten today. Was Cecil okay yesterday?"

"He has some cracked ribs—it seems he was kicked pretty hard. He isn't walking. And he didn't eat today. Probably it's being separated from Franny. I'm keeping an eye on him; let's hope he'll be fine. Eventually one of my techs might take him home."

Maggie went to wash her face and reapply her makeup.

Once they were in Danny's Avalon, driving north on River Road, Danny opened the sun roof to let in the cool evening breeze off the water. "Let me know if it's too much," he said.

"It feels good," Maggie said. She closed her eyes and relaxed into the seat. She had stunned herself by crying so hard. She knew her eyes were still puffy, but Danny didn't seem to mind.

"How far is the restaurant?" she asked.

"Just about a half hour's drive," he said. "You can close your eyes and rest; we don't have to talk on the way." He squeezed her shoulder.

Maggie's mind flashed back to the image of Franny lying on the floor. She felt a contraction in her diaphragm and, afraid she was going to cry again, began taking deep breaths and letting them out silently, hoping Danny wouldn't notice. He had turned the satellite radio to a classical station playing Beethoven's "Moonlight Sonata." Maggie found it calming.

The road along the river was two lanes and dark, although

the moon was almost full. Maggie opened her eyes and smiled at Danny as he pulled into the parking lot.

"I'm so glad we're doing this," Maggie said. "I've missed you very much, even though it's only been a week since we were together." He leaned over to give her a lingering kiss, which she returned. After a few minutes, he said, "We'd better go in, Mags; we'll lose our reservation."

Maggie admired the plush interior, mahogany walls, brass trimmings, and red velvet cushions of the restaurant, all suggesting the features of an elegant 19th-century steamboat. The hostess seated them at a table on the outside deck facing the river. Maggie ordered a glass of Pinot Grigio and grilled salmon and summer vegetables; Danny chose a craft beer and the captain's platter with crab legs, fried cod, and shrimp. Danny looked at Maggie with a half-smile that said, "I'm sorry this is so hard." She smiled back and reached across the table to take his hand. He gave it a squeeze, but neither of them spoke for a minute. Maggie looked out at the water, and Danny watched her face.

"You know I worry about you," he said.

"You don't need to," she replied. "I'm perfectly fine. Yesterday was a shock, but I'm okay— just more determined than ever to find out what's behind this. I feel pretty certain that Franny's death wasn't an accident and that somebody was in her house that night looking for those papers. I have a feeling the answer is in the documents."

"Does anybody know that you have them?" Danny asked.

"I don't know," Maggie said. "Jesse said he was there to get some things he had left in the attic, but then he left without going upstairs." She paused. "I just can't shake the feeling that all these threads are connected somehow."

She lowered her voice.

"I found some actual Keats poems among the papers, and part of a letter. Also, there's the letter from Oscar Wilde that has to have been written to Emma Keats Speed. Then there are the two plantations, Farmington and Endymion, and the friendship between Joshua Speed and Lincoln.

"So today I went to Farmington and learned a lot about Lincoln's visit there. Apparently he had become deeply depressed in the winter of 1841. It worried his friends so much that they didn't want to leave him alone. He stopped attending legislative sessions and kept to his room for nearly six months. Joshua Speed later said they were 'alarmed for his life.' What I've read suggests that Emma and the Speed sisters did a lot to raise Lincoln's spirits. I think Franny's death has something to do with the Speeds."

"All I ask is that you be careful, Mags," Danny said. "If someone murdered that young actor or Franny for something in those chests, I don't want them coming after you next. Do you think maybe you should just give the documents to Jimmy Callahan and leave the whole business alone?" His tone was pleading.

"Are you kidding me? Jimmy wouldn't know what to do with those papers. I think I can figure this out, and I want to figure it out, for everybody's sake," Maggie insisted.

Maggie changed the subject, asking about Danny's daughter Lynn. He said it had been a good visit but lamented that his adult daughter was starting to treat him like a child.

"She raises the volume of her voice as if I'm going deaf and says, 'Dad, Dad, be careful of the curb. Watch where you're going.' It's annoying."

He didn't see any irony in the situation, so Maggie let that lie.

By this time the sun had set and they had finished dinner. The night air on the river was not just cool but damp, and Maggie was getting a chill. She suggested that they either move inside or head home. Danny agreed they should leave.

They were both quiet on the way home. The evening hadn't ended with an argument, but Danny's insistence that Maggie be careful was matched by her insistence that she wasn't in any danger. A white moon reflected on the water outside the passenger window. Maggie fell into a reverie from childhood: that the moon was following her. She remembered summer evenings riding in the back seat of the car, fixing her eyes on the moon and feeling as if she were tethered to it. She thought again of Franny and then of her mother, with a spasm of pain in her throat, and it seemed that the moonlight was bathing the river and the moving treetops in lucent sadness.

–28–

This Fell Sergeant, Death

Wednesday promised to be a cloudless, sunny day in Hagan's Crossing, and Maggie dressed in a pair of black linen slacks and a white linen shirt. She chose a pair of low heels to dress up a little because she would be meeting Ellen Babcock at 11:00. Ellen had flown to Louisville and was renting a car to come for her aunt's funeral. Maggie planned to take her to lunch and to Franny's—now Ellen's—house on Woodbine.

The cats were fed and sitting happily in the sunroom windows when Maggie went out the back door. Amanda Filcher was in her lettuce patch again, this time uprooting the plants that had disappointed her. Maggie waved but slipped into the car quickly because she didn't have time for a chat. *Amanda's a good soul,* she thought, *and she means well. After all this is past, I ought to help her a little more with her genealogy.*

On her route to the motel, Maggie passed a small park that she particularly loved at the beginning of summer. It was planted in crabapple trees and tulip poplars, both of which were in full bloom. The tulip trees, designated as the

Kentucky state tree, were tall and full, with green, white, and orange tulip-shaped flowers high in the branches, yielding a citrusy smell. The crabapples, much shorter and planted around the periphery, were a riot of candy-scented pink blossoms. Maggie stopped under the shade of the trees and rolled down her window. The park was catty-corner to the parking lot of the Carter House Hotel, and Maggie was surprised to see the man she had met in the park hurriedly packing his trunk—actually more tossing than packing, she thought. She recognized him because he was wearing the same beige linen suit and pink shirt he had worn the previous Thursday. She thought about calling out to him to ask about the person he'd talked to in the hotel lobby, but before she could get out of her car, he pulled out and sped away so quickly that he left a strip of rubber on the drive.

Maggie went on to the Fairfield. Ellen Babcock was checking in at the desk when Maggie entered. She was an attractive young woman, Maggie thought, dressed very much as if she were going to court, in a navy suit and white blouse, her blonde hair pulled back from her triangular face and fixed in a braided bun.

When Ellen was finished, Maggie approached and introduced herself, suggesting that Ellen should get settled in her room and then they could go for lunch and to the house. Ellen agreed, and Maggie said she would wait in the lobby.

To her surprise, Maggie looked up a few minutes later to see Marshall Hardy standing at the counter. Had he noticed her sitting there? Why was Marshall asking questions of the desk clerk? He stood there about three minutes and left without looking at her. She pondered how she might discover what he had been asking.

Leave well enough alone, Maggie, said her mother's voice in her head.

I know, Mama, she thought, *but we've gone too far for that.*

Walking up to the desk clerk, she smiled and said, "Excuse me, a friend of mine just checked into the hotel, and I think I just saw someone else who was supposed to meet us asking you a question. Did he ask you about Ellen Babcock?"

The clerk said nothing.

Maggie asked, "Did you give him her room number?"

"No, ma'am. I told him I couldn't confirm any information about our guests. It's part of our privacy policy." He looked flustered. "I can't share information with you either."

"That's okay. Thanks."

When Ellen reappeared in the lobby, Maggie decided she should tell her about Marshall and his possible interest in some of Franny's papers. On the way to lunch, she gave Ellen the background. She concluded with a word of caution.

"Marshall won't hurt you, but he might approach you in the next few days. Just tell him you don't have any trunks or documents."

"Should I tell him you have them?"

"No, I think he'll figure that out."

After lunch at the Cup 'n Saucer, where Maggie and Ellen chose a menu for the post-funeral luncheon, they drove to Franny's house.

"It's even more beautiful than in the photo," Ellen said.

Thankfully all the crime scene tape had been removed, and Maggie had two new sets of keys to give Ellen. Upstairs and down, they explored every room, and Ellen marveled at the antiques. In Franny's bedroom, Ellen picked up the worn copy of the *Book of Common Prayer* from the night table.

"There was one of these in my father's things, given to me when I was in high school," she said. She opened the cover and read out loud the inscription on the flyleaf: "The Lord preserve thy going out and thy coming in. Ps 121 ~ Father."

"My father's has the exact same inscription," Ellen said. "My grandfather must have given both as gifts at the same time."

Ellen took the prayer book and Franny's purse and bankbooks with her. Getting into Maggie's car, she expressed her gratitude for the help, saying again how she felt ill-equipped. Maggie was reassuring Ellen when she was distracted by a car parked on the corner of Willow and Woodbine. Driving past, she didn't see anybody inside.

But why was the maroon car still there?

-29-

It Ends a Mortal Woe

As soon as she had dropped Ellen at the hotel, Maggie called Jimmy's cellphone. He answered on the second ring.

"Yes, Maggie?"

"Just a couple of things I thought you should know. After I met Ellen at the Fairfield, I was waiting in the lobby while she got settled in her room. I looked up to see Marshall Hardy asking the desk clerk questions. I don't think he noticed me sitting there, because there are so many ficus trees. The clerk wouldn't confirm it to me, but I'm pretty sure Marshall was asking about Ellen. Also, Mr. Lindauer's Chevy is still parked on Willow Avenue, facing Woodbine. I was driving past, and it looked empty, but I don't know for sure."

"Huh," Jimmy said. "I let Lindauer go about 3:00 a.m. Tuesday morning. I told him to stay in town, but I guess it's odd that his vehicle hasn't moved in more than 48 hours. I'll send someone by to check on it."

"Anything from the crime lab about Franny's death?"

"Still waiting for the ME, but they did find a button that was apparently torn off of a jacket and got wedged in the bottom of the window channel. They're trying to lift a print."

"What's the button look like?"

"Look like? Wait, lemme see my notes. Um, it's metal, silver, um, with 'Lucky Brand' printed on it. It's the top part—must have lost the tack," he said.

"Well, it's something," Maggie said.

Jimmy changed the subject, asking lots of questions about Ellen Babcock and the plans for the funeral home visitation and the funeral. Maggie satisfied his curiosity and predicted there would be a large crowd.

When she arrived home, Maggie made another call, to Danny. He said that Cecil had sustained some serious internal injuries on Sunday night.

"At first I only saw cracked ribs, but a second X-ray showed a more seriously fractured rib, which then lacerated the liver. He's not doing well," Danny said. "Don't know if the little guy's gonna make it."

"I hope all dogs do go to heaven, then," Maggie said. "I'd like to imagine him reunited with Franny."

Danny suggested they go to dinner again soon; Maggie replied that she would like that too, as soon as these murders were solved. His voice registered irritation as he reminded her she was not a member of the detective squad.

"I *know*, Dan."

He heard the hint of a rebuff in her calling him "Dan" but ignored it. Still, he thought—not for the first time—that he was not going to change this woman, no matter how hard he tried.

They hung up cordially enough, and Maggie took up the topic with the cats, who were lounging nearby, both grooming themselves. They listened with their usual sangfroid and offered no suggestions.

"I guess I'll follow your example and not let him get to me," she said.

Just after supper, Maggie was putting laundry into the washer when she realized the phone was ringing; the sound had been masked by the water. She was out of breath when she answered. It was Jimmy.

"Maggie—are you all right?"

"Yes—just running for the phone. What's up?"

"More bad news. Eddie Lindauer was found dead—lying on his left side—in the backseat of his car. Probably there since Tuesday. It might be the same cause of death as Ron Spear—the ME found evidence of a lot of liquid having been poured into his ear; they're testing to see if it is the same compound."

"Oh Lord, Jimmy—three people in one week! This will raise a panic in town."

"I'd like to keep it quiet for a bit," Jimmy said, "to get a handle on whether they're all connected." Jimmy described that someone could have opened the back door on the driver's side of the Chevy and poured the substance into the sleeping man's ear. It could have been done in a few seconds.

"Now we have another crime scene to process—without final results from the last one," he said. His frustration was contagious. Maggie didn't know what to say.

After ending the call, she went to finish loading the washer and stopped to think. What was it that Eddie Lindauer had written in the note to Jesse?

"You'll be sorry."

-30-

We Are Time's Subjects

The parking lot of Anderson's Funeral Home was so crowded that Maggie had to circle the block and find a spot on a side street. She had come with Ellen earlier in the day before the visitation began as well; there was no other family, and Maggie thought it would be awful for the young woman to go alone through the experience of seeing her deceased aunt. After the first hour, just as visitors began to arrive, Maggie had popped home to put out extra food for the cats and change into more comfortable shoes. She had forgotten how much standing one does in a funeral home.

Franny's visitation was turning out to be the social event her lawyer had predicted. Ellen was already exhausted, and people stood in a receiving line that wound around the room, down the hall, and nearly out the door. Since everybody seemed to know everybody else, people mingled and talked with their neighbors even after they had given Ellen Babcock their condolences. It seemed to Ellen that people kept coming in, but no one was going out.

As Maggie entered the funeral home, the scent of dozens of floral arrangements newly delivered, heavy with fragrant carnations, nearly took her breath away. She spotted Ellen standing near the open casket, looking stricken, not by grief but by the onslaught of people squeezing her hands and hugging her. She had confided to Maggie that she dreaded the ritual of being consoled by hundreds of strangers for a loss she didn't feel.

"I feel like a charlatan, having this funeral," she said.

"I know it's stressful," Maggie said, "but you are honoring a woman who was well respected—and loved—in Hagan's Crossing. Other people will supply the grief. Plus, you can consider it a tribute to your ancestors."

"I guess you're right," Ellen conceded. "It's not really about me."

Maggie made her way through the crowd to stand for a moment in front of the casket. Franny looked peaceful and surprisingly pretty in a blue dress with a Battenburg lace collar. Maggie thought of their lunch on the porch, realizing it had been exactly a week ago—just last Friday. She pressed her lips together in a gesture of resolve and whispered, "I'll find out the truth, Franny. I promise."

Ellen saw her nearby and reached out her hand, inviting Maggie to stand with her.

"Have you taken a break?" Maggie asked. "Why not go into the lounge and sit down for 20 minutes? I can stay here and greet people. Get some coffee or something to eat."

Ellen nodded and threaded herself through the crowd while Maggie turned to the next person in line, Edie Miller, editor of the *Clarion.* While they commiserated on the shock of Franny's passing, Maggie surveyed the room, making mental notes about the interactions she saw. Several members of Franny's birders' group had assembled near the door: Betty and Roger Craig, Lorene Spencer, and Marshall Hardy.

Maggie saw that people were lining up to sign the book of condolences, after which some left and others stayed. When Ellen returned to the room, Marshall approached her, took her elbow, and guided her into the next room, where there were fewer people. Maggie could see him gesturing to Ellen and her shaking her head in the negative. Ellen backed away as Marshall pressed closer to her. Finally she turned and walked away—out into the hallway. Marshall followed her.

Maggie followed too.

In the corridor, Ellen stood with her back against a wall, Marshall once again gesticulating in her face. Maggie approached.

"I was worried about you, Ellen. Is everything all right?" She smiled at both of them and added, "Hi, Marshall. I see you've met Franny's niece."

Marshall muttered a hello and said he had to go. He walked away swiftly.

Ellen looked ready to cry.

"What was that about?" Maggie asked.

"He started telling me that there were items in Aunt Franny's possession that belonged to him—papers in some trunks—and he wanted to get them from me. I told him I would wait for the reading of the will to determine what her possessions were, and if she had left him anything, he would find out then. He said the will didn't matter—that what was his was his. I reminded him that I'm an attorney, but he ignored that. Is he crazy or something?"

"In my book, he's a little eccentric—you never know exactly what's going on with him. If you're ready, let's go back inside." Maggie gave Ellen a sideways hug and led the way back to the spot near the casket.

In the last hours of the calling, the crowd remained steady. Mary Lou came in, and Maggie confirmed the plans for the luncheon after the funeral and burial the next day. Just before she left, Maggie went to the book people had signed and flipped back to the page that interested her. She took a picture on her phone.

Maggie encouraged Ellen to return to the hotel and get a good night's sleep.

"Only one more day," she said. "Only one more day."

31

Speak Less Than Thou Knowest

The days were still lengthening as June continued to pull the Earth around the sun toward the summer solstice. When Maggie left the funeral home, she drove to Central Park, thinking that if she sat a while in front of the stage and went over the opening night of *Hamlet* in her mind, she might remember . . . *Remember what, Maggie?* She couldn't put her finger on what else was missing.

Anna had said that Jesse saw someone he recognized that night, someone "dangerous," so did that explain why he'd left the park? He'd been there for the warm-ups, but he hadn't been seen in his costume. So how early had he left? And who was the man in the black windbreaker? Had she seen a man in black?

"Yes, of course. Everyone backstage was wearing black, Maggie." She spoke to herself with frustration.

She went over in her mind the sequence of events the night of the play. She had seen Mr. Lindauer backstage—and he had blended in with all the other black-clothed people—was he wearing a windbreaker? She couldn't be sure—she was only certain about the Cleveland ball cap. Jimmy Callahan was frustrated that he couldn't charge Lindauer with the murder of Ron Spear. It struck Maggie as unrealistic that Lindauer would go backstage with the intent to kill Jesse while sporting a big red-faced Indian on his head. He might have had a motive and the skill to put together the poison, but something didn't feel right about the idea of Lindauer as a murderer.

Who else had she seen at the play? Last Saturday's paper had run a front-page article with a few pictures. With the focus on the murder, Edie Miller hadn't run a lot of festive-looking shots.

It occurred to Maggie that tomorrow's *Clarion* might contain more. But why wait for that? She took out her cell and called Edie.

Edie answered on the first ring and they talked for a minute about the large crowd at the funeral home. Then Edie confirmed that scores of photos had been taken of the audience on opening night.

"I was planning a big spread, but it didn't seem right after that boy's dying," Edie said.

Maggie asked if she might come by the newspaper office and take a look.

"Sure, I'm just putting the paper to bed; you can come sift through all the pictures taken at the park last week. I can even offer you a cup of coffee," Edie said.

The corner where the *Clarion* office stood had once been dominated by an inn destroyed by fire in the early 1900s. Reminders of its grandeur remained in a cast-iron hitching post in the shape of a large black horse head alongside sandstone mounting steps. Maggie parked on the street opposite the building. As she got out of her car, what she saw caught her breath.

In front of her, the second and third floors of the hotel were ablaze, and the sounds of breaking glass and screams pierced the smoky air. The figure of a woman wrapped in flames appeared for a moment in the top corner window, then seemed to fall from sight. Her screams echoed, as if she had not one but several voices.

The screams persisted even after the vision faded. Shaken by the experience, Maggie slid back into the front seat of the Prius.

"Will I ever get used to this?" she asked aloud. She sat a minute with her eyes closed, taking deep breaths, wondering why this image had come.

Maggie locked her car, crossed the deserted street, and knocked at the door. Edie welcomed her with a hug. They made small talk while Edie poured two cups of coffee.

"Hey, Edie—on my way in, I was reminded of the fire—and your supposed ghost. Have you ever heard anything ghostly here?"

Edie laughed. "No, of course not. Do you think I would hang around here at night if I had a ghost? That's just a great story for tourists. Although . . ."

"Although what?"

"Well, recently some things have been moved around, and I can't imagine who would have done it. I have some bound copies of the early issues of the *Clarion,* kept on a high shelf in the back of the press room. The other morning I found one on the floor—opened to the story of the fire. I guess the ghost could knock it down, but not put it back up," Edie said.

"I'd like to see it. Is the book still down from the shelf?"

"Sure it is. Hold on."

Edie left and came back carrying a huge book: 100 broadsheet issues of the paper, bound in rough leather.

"I can't believe the size of that—oh, be careful, Edie," Maggie said.

"It is heavy, and more than a little dusty," Edie said, dropping it onto a side table.

Maggie shook her head. "Sometime we'll have a conversation about the importance of archiving and preservation, but for now, if you show me the article—and the photos—you can get back to your work. I don't want the paper late tomorrow because of me!"

Maggie sat down to read. The cause of the fire had been traced to the third-floor bedroom in which the young woman had died. Suspicion fell on the man who had claimed to be her husband. They had arrived supposedly from Virginia, the man boasting around town that he was going to start a distillery in the area. They had been in residence nine days, however, when the man got involved in a high-stakes card game, losing nearly all his money and getting blind drunk as a consequence.

He had then argued bitterly with his wife—and, it was conjectured, locked her in the room after knocking over a paraffin lamp and starting the fire. He fled and was never found, and the hotel was damaged beyond repair.

Maggie stared at the name—Joseph Gilmer.

"I do not believe in coincidence," she murmured to herself.

Then she turned to the stack of photographs Edie had assembled. With a magnifying glass, Maggie identified nearly every audience member, finding at the back of the house the figure of Eddie Lindauer in a black windbreaker and Cleveland Indians cap. In another shot, she recognized Marshall Hardy near the concession stand. Why had Marshall made a point of saying he wasn't there?

Maggie finished with the photos and thanked Edie. On her way home, she decided on another piece of genealogy she wanted to check.

Once in the house, ignoring the effusive welcome from the cats, she opened her laptop and searched through the census records from 1910 and 1920. Then she turned to the Ohio birth records. It didn't take long for her to discover the answer to her question.

Now, what to do about it?

–32–

Life's Fitful Fever

The sun was setting over the bend in the river when the young man knocked on the screen door. Footsteps echoed from the back of the house, and for a few seconds, he almost regretted coming.

The man who came to the door was wearing summer-weight slacks and an oxford cloth dress shirt.

He grunted a greeting at the visitor and pushed the screen door open.

"Why so dressed up?" the young man asked.

"Funeral home," he replied.

"What did you find out?"

"Nothing."

They both walked into the kitchen, the younger man going to the refrigerator and taking out a beer. They faced each other across the table.

"Glad to know you feel at home enough to help yourself," the older man said. His frown and the edge on his voice made his visitor uncomfortable. "Speaking of which, the last time you were here it seems you helped yourself to something else. I noticed it was missing, and I wondered what you were up to. You'd better be careful."

The younger man took a long drink from the bottle before

denying he had taken anything at all. They looked at each other silently, warily, with the weight of the unsaid hanging in the air.

"Do you understand me?" the older man added at last. "Don't get careless. Don't implicate me in—in anything."

"Me? Careless? Give me a break. You're the bungler," said the younger. He leaned in, stared hard at the older man, and spoke slowly, emphasizing every word: "I know what you did." Then he leaned back. "Besides, what do you expect me to do now? You can't blame me for your mistakes."

"I didn't make any mistakes—except for involving you, maybe. You didn't move fast enough, and I think you may have double-crossed me. I heard there was a guy in town looking to buy documents. Now, how did he come into the picture?"

Again the younger man denied knowing anything about it. He straightened his shoulders and stared coldly. As the older man became more agitated, shifting in his seat, his face reddening, the younger man grew more still and more focused.

"Does the niece have the documents?" he asked.

"That's what you're supposed to tell me, kiddo."

The older man got up from the table, slapping it angrily, and leaned into the other man's face.

"Damn, you're worthless. Not the boy wonder your mother thought you'd become," he spat. "You've bungled this whole thing."

"Don't you *ever* mention my mother. *Ever. Again.*" This shout was accompanied by a shove that sent the older man reeling against the kitchen sink. For a moment, it seemed the younger man might hit him with an upraised fist, and the older man reached back across the counter to find a weapon, but then they just stopped. They were both breathing hard.

The visitor resumed his seat.

"What happened to that Lindauer guy?" the older man asked.

"Dunno. Left town, I guess," the young man said. After a tense silence he added, "So, what now?"

"Maggie O'Malley. She knows something. And she's gonna keep digging around."

"Yeah. Okay." The younger man finished the beer in one long swig, got up from the table, and walked to the front door. "I'll be in touch," he said, letting the screen door slam behind him.

33

Rounded With a Sleep

On Saturday morning Franny's funeral took place as expected, with several hundred residents of Hagan's Crossing crammed into the small Episcopal chapel next to McLaughlin College. Her prominence in the community, the rumor that she had died from some "misadventure," and the appearance of a hitherto unknown niece had resulted in an event no one wanted to miss. Franny had planned the service in advance, a blessing to her niece, who wasn't a churchgoer and would have had no idea where to start. Maggie was grateful too, since she was so preoccupied with the mystery of Franny's death that it was difficult to focus on the funeral.

The hearse and limousine, followed by a parade of cars, drove slowly from the east end of town, where the chapel was, to the far west end, where the Holy Angels Cemetery sprawled over several hills and valleys carved from Kentucky limestone. Its oldest inhabitants were members of the Hagan family, including Thomas, whose name had been virtually erased by 200 years of wind and rain. But a family monument bearing the Hagan crest verified his residence. The winding avenues that linked section to section were lined by mature shade trees: tulip poplar, pin oak, and maple.

It was almost noon when the mourners finally assembled around Franny's open grave. The Episcopal priest opened with the modern rite for burial in the *Book of Common Prayer*, then read a passage from Lamentations: "The steadfast love of the Lord never ceases, his mercies never come to an end." As he prayed, Maggie's attention fell on the headstones around her, the graves of Franny's parents, grandparents, great- and great-great-grandfathers. She thought of the papers in her den that these people had once held and read, even created.

A gust of wind caused her to look up over the shoulder of the priest, where she saw a pale man in workman's clothes seeming to lean casually on a large, waist-high monument. *What's the gravedigger doing there?* she thought. *So close. Like he can't wait to fill it in. That's awful.* Another gust blew the program out of her hand, and when she stood up from retrieving it, she saw the man was gone.

When the readings and prayers had ended, the priest signaled that people might throw some dirt or a flower into the grave while he read:

> *In sure and certain hope of the resurrection to eternal life through our Lord Jesus Christ, we commend to Almighty God our sister Frances, and we commit her body to the ground; earth to earth, ashes to ashes, dust to dust. The Lord bless her and keep her, the Lord make His face to shine upon her and be gracious to her, the Lord lift up his countenance upon her and give her peace. Amen.*

Maggie's eyes filled with tears as she dropped dirt onto the casket, the thud of it sounding louder than it should. She took a long-stemmed pink rose from the basket provided and walked toward the place where she had seen the gravedigger. The stone he had leaned on was facing away from her, and she had to walk through several rows of graves and around some large azalea bushes to reach its front. The inscription surprised her: "Elijah Marshall Hardy, 1838–1898."

Was that Marshall's great-grandfather I saw leaning on the grave? she wondered. *What would he have to tell me?*

A few steps away she found a stone marked "Edward William Hardy, 1888–1963," and behind that another that read "William Elijah Hardy, 1920–1971." That, she knew, was Marshall's father. He had died when Marshall was 20 or 21—an event that almost caused the son to drink himself out of graduating from college. Maggie remembered the uproar Marshall had caused the night after his father was buried—a physical fight in the center of town with his younger sister, a public display that landed him in jail overnight. He drank heavily all that summer but pulled it together and finally finished undergrad and a pharmacy degree.

Maggie was scribbling the information from the gravestones down in a small notebook when Marshall came up behind her.

"What do you think you're doing, Maggie?"

She turned abruptly. What flashed into her mind was the scene in the movie *2001: A Space Odyssey* when HAL, the computer, questions Dave, who is trying to disable him.

"I'm taking some notes. It's genealogy."

"My genealogy?"

"Why not? Your family has lived in Hagan's Crossing for generations. You said yourself that your grandfather used to tell you stories about what went on around Endymion."

"I haven't asked you to research my family," he said, moving closer to her.

Maggie turned to face him and took a step backward.

"You don't own the past, even the history of your own family. The truth has a pesky way of coming out no matter what."

The rest of the mourners had already walked back to their cars, well out of earshot, and for a moment, looking into Marshall's eyes, Maggie was afraid.

He turned on his heels—muttering "Damn nosy bitch"—and stalked to his pickup truck. Maggie stood and watched him drive away, then finished copying the names and dates from the gravestones.

The cemetery ground was uneven and Maggie was wearing heels, so she walked slowly back to her own car, seeing that Jimmy Callahan had pulled up behind her and was standing with his back to the driver's door.

"I have a coroner's report on Miss Babcock's death," he said.

"And?"

Jimmy pulled a folded report out of his inner coat pocket.

"A spiral fracture of the left humerus with deep bruising. A fractured skull—damage to the occipital area of the head and intracranial injuries. It seems she was grabbed by the upper arm, and it was twisted before she was pushed backward down the steps," he said.

Maggie shook her head. For once, she had no words.

–34–

Time Shall Unfold

After the funeral luncheon Maggie arrived home at 4:30, exhausted. Like the visitation and the church service, the luncheon had been attended by scores of Franny's friends and neighbors. Maggie felt as if she had been talking nonstop for two days, and she welcomed the silence of her cool, empty house. Danny had wanted to come over for the evening, but Maggie had begged off, promising next week. The cats welcomed her at the door, expecting treats, and Maggie complied before collecting the mail and sinking into her favorite chair.

In planning the luncheon, Maggie had seen to it that Franny's presence was palpable. Every table in the hall held a vase of her beloved blue hydrangeas. A collage of pictures traced her early life, and several people stood to share memories of Franny. Ellen Babcock concluded the event by thanking everyone for their kindness and asking them to take some flowers home in remembrance of her aunt.

Now Maggie had been sitting and thinking, doodling on the notebook in front of her for so long that she hadn't realized the sun had set. Glancing at the large wooden trunks across the room, she thought how much they resembled two coffins tucked into the shadows. "Makes sense," she said aloud. "They're full of the fragments of dead people's lives."

She had been mulling over a letter she had received earlier that day from a dead man: Avery Prendergast.

Prendergast had explained he was writing to her because she might be the person who could find and save a valuable document. She remembered meeting him on the opening night of *Hamlet*. Apparently, he had taken down her name because of that conversation.

So much had happened since that meeting. Ron Spear had been killed, Jesse Gilemorane— really Gilmer—had disappeared, then reappeared, then disappeared again, and strangest of all, Franny had been pushed to her death. Eddie Lindauer had probably been poisoned. Four deaths inside a week. Maggie didn't think Hagan's Crossing had ever seen such a string of tragedies. She thought about seeing Avery Prendergast packing his car on Wednesday morning outside the Carter House Hotel. She reread aloud from the letter:

I freely admit, Ms. O'Malley, that I was invited here to Hagan's Crossing by someone I had corresponded with to assist them in getting possession of a fragment of a priceless document. I was offered a tremendous sum of money to get that document from Miss Babcock. I even explored her back porch the day I visited her, to see if I could easily get into her house. I couldn't. But I did not kill her, and since she has died, and I do not want suspicion to fall on me, I am leaving town. I am only making one stop to purchase an unrelated document—and then I will be gone. I think, however, that you are in danger because of the historical papers believed to be in your possession. I cannot prove it, but I think the young man who hired me has already killed someone. I would hate for you to be next.

After she had initially read this undated letter, Maggie had called Jimmy.

"Oh, no," he'd said upon hearing Prendergast's name. "You're kidding me. We just found his body in the front seat of his car on a gravel road up near the river. A passing motorist thought it looked abandoned, and the left rear bumper was sticking out. It looked like it had been glanced by a passing car."

"How did he die?" Maggie had asked.

"Stabbed in the heart. The ME says he's been dead a number of days. Flies were laying eggs. Wallet was empty, but his auto registration in the glove compartment gave us a name. Another quarter mile into the woods we found a small cabin with some signs of recent use. Forensics is gathering evidence. I'm hoping to find some fingerprints or DNA."

"Any suspects?"

"Not yet. I'm gonna need that letter, though. The 'young man' detail is interesting."

Maggie's phone rang, bringing her back to the present. She still kept a landline as well as her cell phone, which she knew was borderline Luddite behavior, but she had a fondness for the number and liked having both. The caller was Mary Lou, talking very quickly about having found something else in the chifforobe belonging to Cassie.

"Can you come over, Mags? I found another compartment in the bottom drawer."

Maggie agreed. Pulling on her raincoat because a storm was in the forecast, she turned on lights in the kitchen, living room, and her bedroom. She checked the sunroom door, closing the vertical blinds, and went out the front door to her car. Backing out of the drive, Maggie thought she might need to schedule some tree trimming on the oak and maples that stretched their highest branches across the right side of the gabled roof of her Craftsman bungalow with its wide front porch and triple dormer windows.

Mary Lou met Maggie at the door with tears in her eyes. Wordlessly, she led Maggie into a back room of the basement and turned on the light, revealing a six-foot oak chifforobe with a door on the right for hanging items and a smaller door with seven drawers on the left.

"It's beautiful, Mary Lou! What a wonderful antique!" Maggie said. "Do you know what it's made of?"

"It's quarter-sawn oak, very well made. That little door on the top left is for hats or bonnets, and the two small drawers are for handkerchiefs or hosiery." She opened the door on the right and squatted to pull out what seemed to be the floor of the closet section.

"This turns out to be a false bottom," Mary Lou said. "And look."

She stood up and handed Maggie a small package. Loosely wrapped in another piece of dressmaker's tissues bearing a written note from Cassie was a small, yellowed handkerchief, folded into a triangle and embroidered with the name *Emma.*

"It may be something Cassie made for her," Mary Lou said.

Maggie was silent for a moment. Then, holding the handkerchief, she whispered, "Cassie . . ."

. . . and a flood of images surrounded her, as in a kaleidoscope: Akosua on the ship in chains, Athena clinging to Cassie, Cassie cradling Joseph's bloody head. The tears—all the tears shed by these women—welled up inside her. She did not cry herself but sat down with the weight of their collective sorrow.

"What is it, Maggie? Are you all right?" Mary Lou looked alarmed. "You're so very pale."

"Yes." The vision had passed. "Yes, I'm okay." She gave the paper and handkerchief back to Mary Lou, who sat down on a couch beside her.

"What does the note say?" Maggie asked.

"That's what made me cry," Mary Lou said. She read from the faded tissue: "Miss Emma don't know I remember my mama Athena, but I do. When I was a little girl dressed up in a lacy dress with ribbons, I saw my mama watchin' me. And when we went away, Miss Emma was a mama to me, until—until—of course, she never was. Oh, I'm an old woman now, and how I miss my mama."

"Wow," Maggie said. They sat for a moment in silence. "Mary Lou, this is a wonderful treasure. I'm sure there's more to know."

"Can I get you anything? Tea? Hot or cold?" Mary Lou asked.

"No—thanks—there's a big thunderstorm in the forecast, we're under a tornado watch, and it sounds as if the rain has already started. I'd like to get home before the wind gets too strong."

On the way upstairs they chatted about how nice the luncheon had been and how pleased Ellen had been with it. Mary Lou stood at the door to watch Maggie leave, but then the car didn't move.

Maggie got out and darted back to the house as hail began pelting her.

"My car won't start. I should have had it checked. This happened a couple of days ago too."

"Don't worry. No problem," Mary Lou said. "I still have to go to the bank to make my night deposit. I'll drop you at home, and we can sort your car out tomorrow. Just let me get my things."

When they pulled up to Maggie's house, Mary Lou leaned over to give her friend a hug.

"Thank you, Mags. Thank you for leading me to Cassie."

Maggie said, "No, it's Cassie who's done all the leading."

Maggie ran to the house as a streak of lightning struck perilously close. Once inside she dried off and changed into a cozy pair of sweats. The cats, who followed her into the bedroom, seemed to agree that a rainstorm could give you a chill even on a June night.

Mary Lou, meanwhile, was taking it slowly in the driving rain, even wondering if she should postpone going to the bank until morning. Around the corner from Maggie's house, she noticed a pickup truck pulled off the road, partly shrouded in foliage. *Is that Marshall Hardy? What's he doing sitting there?* she thought. She slowed down even more.

It was Marshall. In her rearview mirror she could see the soaring white bird in the circular logo of the American Birding Association, illuminated by lightning on the back panel of his truck.

She decided to go ahead to the bank after all.

Maggie went back into the den with the trunks and took out the Keats papers she had stored away. She also went through her files, rereading what she had recorded about

Farmington and the history of the Endymion property. In census records, she had identified all the Speed family members and employees after the war years. This had led her to newspaper stories following up on the robbery and clues about exactly what had been stolen. For a while after Mary Lou had gone, Maggie read through all her notes. Then she turned to the original Keats papers.

—35—

What Plighted Cunning Hides

Examining the document Mary Lou had found, Maggie decided it had been torn during the 1874 robbery. Many of the letters along its left edge had been torn away. The "Aunt Emma" to whom it was addressed was certainly Emma Keats Speed.

Maggie read it again.

Dear Aunt Emma,
Joy is the memory of things
eautiful. Sorrow comes to all,
and Death haunts us, but
beauty will not pass away. Why
is that? Because in the mind
where memory lives, every
rose-tinged sunrise still resides.
Every field of goldenrod forever
waves in an eternal breeze.
othing is lost. Nothing is truly
lost. Memory is a world mid-

ay between heaven and earth.
is "flowery band" I have
ven binds my heart to the
tucky of my birth, and
uty does in fact move the
l from my dark spirits. How
teful I am for the enduring
ht of friendship.

The half signature, although torn, was unmistakable.

ncoln

Realizing that she hadn't explored the last layer of papers in one of the trunks, Maggie returned to the search. Most of the personal papers had been in the bottom of this one trunk, so perhaps there was more to be discovered from the Speeds. It didn't take long for Maggie to extract what she had hoped for. She unfolded the letter carefully. It was dated "Springfield, August 1850."

My Dear Mrs. Speed,
It is with great gratitude that I write to you and enclose the copy of your Uncle John's manuscript which you shared with me some years ago at Farmington. I dare say you might have expected it to be returned sooner, but I have been an itinerant lawyer and in the vagabond way for so long that I forgot my manners. I cannot tell you how much this poetry restored my soul; I read it over every day for months and finally had the courage to make notes of my humble thoughts as you had requested. Those weeks at Farmington indeed wove "a

flowery band" to "bind me to the earth" and the memory of those beautiful summer days surrounded by a loving family removed the shade from my "dark spirits."

Please give my regards to your husband and his family and convey my deepest respect to your mother-in-law, whose kindness in the summer of 1841 afforded me the greatest consolation.

Your Sincere Friend,
A. Lincoln

Maggie realized she had been holding her breath and let out a deep sigh. This half-document Cassie had retrieved—the part the caretaker had not been able to find in the pile of ransacked papers—was indeed valuable. Now she knew, though, that someone had the other half and was willing to kill for what she held in her hand. She folded the letter carefully into another sheet of acid-free paper and put it with the Keats poems and Cassie's note in a locked drawer.

Pulling the notes she had taken in the cemetery from her purse, Maggie went to her laptop and opened several tabs—her subscription to Newspapers.com and two other genealogy websites. She began searching Ohio newspapers and marriage records for the names Gilmer and Hardy. She found more than she expected. Joseph Gilmer, who had fled from the fire in Hagan's Crossing in 1901, fathered a son, Raymond J. Gilmer, in 1915, and Raymond in turn fathered Lawrence Gilmer in 1945. In 1985, when he was 40, Lawrence married Mary Ann Hardy, and she gave birth to a boy, Jesse William Gilmer, in 1988, when she was 35.

So—Jesse was Marshall's nephew.

Maggie had no idea whether Joseph Gilmer had any connection to the Speeds, but it occurred to her that Marshall was so possessed by his family's connection that he might have convinced himself he had a double right to the documents because of his sister's marriage.

In the newspaper archive, she found another bombshell: a story in the Ashland *Times-Gazette* from July 3, 1999, reporting the car accident that had killed Mary Ann.

> *Ashland, Ohio—One woman was killed and a man injured yesterday afternoon when their Ford van hit a concrete embankment on southbound Interstate 71 in Ashland County. A ten-year-old boy was pulled unharmed from the wreckage by motorists who stopped to help.*
>
> *The accident was reported at 2:20 and the highway was closed for three hours. Ohio State Trooper Gerald Hopper identified the woman killed as Ohio resident Mary Ann Gilmer, aged 46.*
>
> *The Ford van was demolished by the impact, and welders were needed to cut the twisted metal under which the woman was pinned. The man, as yet unidentified, was taken to an area hospital with minor injuries.*
>
> *According to Hopper, the cause of the accident is under investigation. Broken beer bottles littered the wreckage, and it has not been determined which adult was driving.*
>
> *"Based on the appearance of the van, which had rolled onto its top, it's surprising there were any survivors," Hopper said.*

Maggie printed out the records she had found. She realized

how hungry she was and went to the kitchen to heat up some leftovers, which she ate standing at the counter. She rinsed the plate and took a glass of Pinot Grigio with her back into the den. She loved the layout of the house, with the den tucked into the back corner and a sunroom spanning most of the back wall, leading into the kitchen and an attached laundry room. The double doors of the sunroom also opened into the kitchen.

The abundance of windows gave plenty of light, and in a huge thunderstorm like this one, she had a front-row seat for the pyrotechnics.

The storm outside had intensified, and the cats had come meowing into the room. Finn, who looked like a lion, was every bit the coward when the thunder shook the house.

"That storm is right overhead," Maggie said to the cats. "Maybe you guys should get up in the chair with me and snuggle under this blanket."

They both recognized the signal when Maggie sat and fluffed the blanket. Finn burrowed under it and Fiona climbed onto Maggie's lap. For her part, Maggie liked the sound of rain on the roof and the scene of the trees twisting and bending in the wind like dancers in a frantic ballet.

Then the lights flickered and went out. She looked out the window to see that the whole street was dark. The streetlights too.

"Oh, darn—I should have put out some candles earlier, Fiona," she said, sliding the cat off her lap. She reached for a flashlight in a nearby drawer and went to the closet for a battery-operated electric lantern.

"It's a good thing I just put new batteries in here," she said to the cat.

In the noise of a branch banging against the back of the

sunroom, Maggie didn't hear the door being jimmied open. Another flash of lightning that struck nearby illuminated the open door for a fraction of a second, and Maggie recognized Marshall Hardy, standing with a crowbar in his hand.

She felt preternaturally calm. For a moment she saw not Marshall but his great-grandfather Elijah, the same man she had seen in the cemetery, brandishing the weapon. She had discovered the connection and knew, now with conviction, that Marshall had inherited the stolen document.

She spoke. "Close the door, would you, Marshall? The rain is blowing in."

He looked stunned by the tone of her greeting, as if he hadn't just broken into her house.

"I thought you weren't here, Maggie." He looked embarrassed. "I'm not here to hurt you—I just want what rightly belongs to me. You know what I mean, Maggie. You should just give it to me, and I'll be on my way."

"Why don't you sit down in the kitchen, Marshall? I'll get you a towel," she said.

"Dammit, Maggie, give me what I came for. I don't want to hurt you."

"I'm glad to hear that," she said, handing him a towel from the nearby laundry room, then sitting with the electric lantern at the kitchen table.

Marshall advanced but didn't sit down.

"Don't fool with me, Maggie."

"I'm not, Marshall. I just think we should talk about this. I know quite a bit about what's been going on. You might be interested to hear it."

He pulled a chair away from the table and straddled it, legs on either side, holding the crowbar with both hands. He was wearing the black denim jacket and jeans he usually wore, and he looked soaked through.

"So, what do you think you know?" he asked.

"I know that you've had a plan to get ahold of certain documents for a long time, and you thought it would be easy to get them from Franny Babcock—with the help of your nephew."

"My nephew?"

"Jesse Gilmer—not Gilemorane—the son of your younger sister Mary Ann. She married the grandson of Joseph Gilmer, a man who was suspected of murdering his wife. Maybe he was a distant relative of the Speeds—and you've been obsessed with the Speeds for years. That's why you wrote to Jesse and invited him to Hagan's Crossing to help you get the document from Franny. I'm sure it's your handwriting on the handbill Franny had posted—"

"Doesn't prove anything," Marshall interrupted.

"But Jesse came with more baggage than you expected, didn't he? A dead boyfriend and a grieving father who followed him to town. Mr. Lindauer started watching Franny's house, waiting for Jesse—whom he had threatened. Did Jesse tell you about that? That Lindauer had sent him a threatening note? He was scared of Lindauer. And I think then you found out the truth about Jesse. You couldn't trust him."

"Whaddya mean by that?" he asked.

"Well, Jesse saw that there was a way to double-cross you. He contacted a man named Prendergast who was coming to an event at McLaughlin College. It must have been a shock for you to run into him and be told he was planning to buy *your* documents."

Marshall made no answer. He stood up and lifted the

electric lantern from the table, placing it on a high shelf that encircled the kitchen.

"That's better. Now we can see. Get me the document, Maggie," he said.

She didn't move.

"Was Franny's death an accident?" Maggie asked.

"How should I know?"

"Because you were *there.* I know you came in Franny's kitchen window. There's a button missing from your jacket. Any idea where it is? It's not very lucky to lose a Lucky Brand button when you're climbing in a window to break into someone's house."

Marshall looked down at his jacket and saw the button was gone.

"You've got that all wrong," he said. "I didn't hurt Franny."

Another close lightning strike, followed by an almost immediate burst of thunder, made both of them jump. Maggie noticed that the cats had climbed onto the high shelf—where they went when they were anxious. Fiona had arched her back and flattened her ears; Finn had inched closer to the edge where the shelf met the doorway and crouched in a hunter's pose.

The sunroom door flew open unexpectedly, as if blown by the wind, but actually pushed by Jesse. The young man was soaking wet, and the scowl on his face was visible in the half-light of the room. He held a gun.

"Did you get the paper?" he demanded of Marshall.

"I told you to stay in the truck," Marshall said.

"I'm done with you tellin' me what to do. I'm doing this *my way,* old man," Jesse said.

Marshall looked shocked but kept his composure.

"Come on, Jesse, I don't want any more violence. Nobody else needs to get hurt. It was bad enough what happened to Franny, for instance. You shouldn't have let her fall down the steps."

Jesse started to laugh. "*Let* her fall? I *made* her fall, you old fool. I was happy to push her, her and that yapping little mongrel," Jesse said.

Maggie let out an unintended gasp.

Jesse sneered at her.

"I was pretty convincing in the part of the 'distraught young man,' wasn't I?"

"Yes," Maggie said, "you had me fooled." She glanced at Marshall. "I think you had everyone fooled, Jesse, but you won't get away with it. You really put on a performance for me in Franny's kitchen. You had me believing you cared about her."

Maggie was scared but hoped she could get Marshall on her side.

"Don't you see, Marshall? Jesse's ace in the hole is blaming you for Franny's death. He had already discovered that the trunks had been removed from her house. That must have infuriated you, Jesse," she said.

"Damn you," Marshall spat at Jesse.

Jesse glared back at him.

"I had everything under control," Jesse said to Marshall. "There was no need for you to follow me to Franny's that night. But since you did—well—you're the one who had the motive to kill her." He laughed again at Marshall's disbelief.

"Marshall—" Maggie began. Jesse interrupted her.

"Now cut the crap, lady, and get the document."

Maggie decided she needed to keep talking.

"He's betrayed you, Marshall."

"He has no reason to betray me. We're blood," Marshall said.

"Yes," Maggie said, "but he blames you for the death of his mother. Did you and she argue over the document with Lincoln's signature? Maybe Mary Ann believed she had more right to it than you because she had married a Gilmer—a man who died and left her a son to raise."

Maggie turned her attention to Jesse. "How did your mother die, Jesse?"

He glared at her but said nothing.

"Who was driving the Ford van, Marshall?" she asked. "I suspect it was you, but you persuaded the police it was Mary Ann. Were you drunk? Were the two of you fighting when you lost control of the van—and Mary Ann was crushed?"

She turned her attention to Jesse, whose face twisted in pain.

"I'm right, aren't I, Jesse? You were just a kid in the backseat. The adults were fighting and drinking. Then your uncle smashed into a concrete embankment and killed your mother. You never forgave him."

"Shut the hell up," Jesse said.

Maggie continued, talking quickly, describing how Marshall had contacted Jesse to help him get the document, promising him a share, and how Jesse had decided to get his revenge.

"Marshall, do you really think Jesse is going to let you keep that Keats/Lincoln document? He hasn't come here tonight to help you. Nothing Jesse's done has been for your benefit," she said.

Marshall's face contorted in pain as he looked at Jesse. He didn't need to ask the question; it was written all over him.

For a moment Jesse hesitated.

"Yeah, that's right, Marshall. When I got to the Shakespeare gig and met Ron, I told him a little about the documents. I knew Prendergast and got him to come to town so we could fence the stuff, but Ron got cold feet—and I had to get rid of him." Jesse laughed. "I knew using some of the poison you had would be good insurance for me. Nice to have a pharmacist in the family."

"How could you, Jesse?" Marshall asked.

"Collateral damage." He aimed the gun at Marshall, saying to Maggie, "Get the papers. Now.

I'm done with this."

Marshall lunged toward Jesse. What happened next was a blur. Jesse fired, hitting Marshall in the belly; Finn, startled by the sound, jumped from the shelf; the electric lantern tipped over and fell onto Jesse's head, knocking him to the ground and causing him to lose hold of the pistol. Maggie started toward the door, but Jesse grabbed her ankle with his left hand, and she went sprawling just as he retrieved the gun with his right hand.

Then another shot rang through the house.

-36-

The Be-All and the End-All

The sunroom door stood wide open, with the wind still blowing in. The lantern, now sideways on the floor, illuminated the bodies, casting eerie shadows on the walls. Standing in the open doorway, frozen in a shooting posture, Mary Lou yelled to Maggie, "Mags, are you okay? Mags?"

Maggie had wrenched her ankle from Jesse's grasp. Getting first onto all fours, she stood up. Then, feeling dizzy, she dropped into a kitchen chair.

"Yes," she said softly, then again loudly. "Yes, I'm okay. Thank God for you, Mary Lou."

Marshall moaned. Mary Lou stepped into the room and kicked Jesse's gun out of his reach. He was holding his right shoulder with his left hand, writhing in pain.

"We should call 9-1-1," Maggie said.

"Already done," Mary Lou said. "They should all be here in a minute."

Almost as soon as she had spoken, they heard the whoop of a

siren in the driveway and Chief Callahan came running around the corner of the house.

"Is anybody hurt?"

He looked startled to see Mary Lou holding her gun. "It was really smart of you to call me, Mary Lou."

The paramedics were right behind him.

Marshall, more critically injured, was taken by the first ambulance on the scene. Mary Lou had shot Jesse in the shoulder. Callahan read him his rights and placed him under arrest before sending him to the hospital with a guard.

"Mary Lou, I'll need your weapon for ballistics, but you'll get it back." She placed the gun in the evidence bag Callahan held open to her. "And we need to get you two to the station and take statements. At least the lights are still on in that part of town. You might not get electricity restored until tomorrow; lightning hit a transformer."

Mary Lou said she would drive separately to the station. Callahan walked Maggie out to the front seat of his patrol car and she buckled herself in. Crime scene officers had gone into the house through the front door.

"Wait. Where are the cats? Did you see them?" Maggie asked.

"No, I didn't."

She bolted from the front seat of the car and ran into the dark house, calling, "Finn! Fiona!" repeatedly. Jimmy followed with the flashlight, and Maggie led him to the tight corner between the dresser and the wall in the back bedroom where she suspected they would be.

"Oh, thank God, there you are. It's all right, you're all right," she said, reaching back to cup Finn's head in her hand and stroke his left ear. "They'll come out when they're ready," she said.

The crime scene team decided they should just lock the house and return in daylight to process the scene.

En route to the station, Jimmy explained that Mary Lou had phoned him to say that Marshall Hardy was parked around the corner when she left, and the more she thought about it, the more it worried her. She had urged Jimmy to go check on Maggie. He had tried calling first, but the phone had gone to voice mail. Then, when he had neared the parked truck, he had seen it was empty and called for backup.

Once in Callahan's office, with a blanket around her and a cup of hot tea, Maggie told the story, explaining how she had deduced that Jesse was behind the murders. Both he and Marshall had told numerous lies, but Jesse had had a motive to frame both Lindauer and Marshall—and his access to poison from Marshall made him a likely suspect for the killing of Ron Spear. She recounted how chilling it was to hear Jesse laugh about having killed Ron and Franny.

Since Marshall still trusted him, she explained, Marshall didn't know that Jesse had planned all along to get Franny's valuable documents for himself. Jesse's slip about Cecil had obviously shaken him. He had almost admitted the dog was badly hurt—and how could he have known that unless he was there after Franny fell? And Prendergast had provided the clue that Jesse might be his murderer in the letter mentioning the "young man" who had hired him.

"I'm sorry to say that Jesse Gilmer is a thoroughly bad person," Maggie said. "I think you'll find the evidence that he killed four people."

"I'll be glad to get him behind bars," Jimmy said. "But I still have questions about what started all this. What's the connection with the trunks of documents and Marshall Hardy?"

Maggie narrated the story of Lincoln's visit to Farmington, the copy of the opening lines of *Endymion* that Emma Keats had given to Lincoln, and the robbery in which the document had been torn. She said that Marshall's lies about owning the property where the old plantation had been intrigued her—why would he lie? It turned out his great-grandfather, Elijah Hardy, had murdered Mary Lou's great-grandfather Joseph Clark. Jimmy expressed amazement that Mary Lou's family was at the center of the puzzle.

"Imagine finding all that in an old chifforobe you might have tossed away," he said to Mary Lou, shaking his head in disbelief.

Mary Lou said she was grateful that Maggie had traced her genealogy and researched the connection between the Lincoln/Keats document and her family.

"I'm the one who's grateful, Mary Lou. What was it that made you come back to my house?"

"I just had a bad feeling about seeing the truck, so after I went to the bank, I drove back to your neighborhood. The lights all being out from the storm worried me, and I drove past your house. I thought I saw more than one figure outlined in the lantern light. That's when I called Jimmy. I parked and walked up your drive and stood in the back yard near the open door, but I could hear only some of what was said." She looked at Callahan. "I was praying you would get there and kicking myself for not calling you sooner. Then I heard the gunshot and pushed the door open. Everyone was on the floor, and Jesse had just picked up his gun, aiming it at Maggie."

"I'm sure you saved my life, Mary Lou," Maggie said. "Thank you."

Mary Lou smiled. "We're both lucky."

It was near midnight, and the storm had passed, but Jimmy confirmed with a phone call that the power was still out at Maggie's house.

"You can't go home until we've processed the scene anyway. Why don't you call Jack and ask him to come get you?" he suggested.

She didn't give him any argument. She was more than ready to be looked after by her big brother for a while.

The next morning Jack fixed the two of them a big breakfast, and they lingered until it was almost noon. Jack had listened to the story with fascination, interrupting with lots of questions, occasionally chiding Maggie for taking too many chances and pointing out that her nosiness would be her undoing. After she had described the tense scene between her, Marshall, and Jesse, Jack looked pensive.

"You know, Mags, what we need is more enjoyment in our lives. We need to travel and make the most of these years. It would kill me to lose you—no, seriously—I mean, life is unpredictable. We need to plan some trips. Like, let's go up to the Derby in Louisville next May and spend the week—you and me—and Danny if you want—and let's plan a trip to Ireland with Anna and Grace. I need to take her to Gráinne O'Malley's castle on Clare Island. Whaddya say?"

For a moment Maggie saw her grandmother Nora

standing in the doorway, smiling at the two of them. Then she was gone.

Standing up, she leaned down and kissed Jack on his brow.

"I kiss you hade," she said. "We'll do it! For now, though, I have some starving cats to feed, so will you give me a ride home?"

Epilogue

Jesse Gilmer was charged with first-degree murder in the deaths of Ron Spear, Franny Babcock, Eddie Lindauer, and Avery G. Prendergast as well as the attempted murder of Marshall Hardy. The bullet from Mary Lou's gun had pierced his brachial plexus, requiring reconstructive surgery. He was sentenced to life in prison without parole.

Marshall Hardy's injuries were to the stomach and small intestine; they also required surgery. He made a full recovery. He was subsequently charged with breaking and entering and being an accessory to the murder of Franny Babcock. Marshall was sentenced to ten years, with the possibility of parole after five years. Feeling remorse for planning to steal the Keats/Lincoln document—and hoping to curry favor with the court—Marshall gave his half of the document to Mary Lou Johnson.

Mary Lou had the document restored and appraised. It was, indeed, the rumored treasure that Cassie had promised, not just a valuable piece of paper but a repository of memories, an inheritance of loss and restoration, and a promise that the past is never past.

Cecil made a full recovery from his injuries and found a happy home with the dog groomer who worked with Danny. Happily, the groomer could make a mean chicken omelet.

Keats's Poem with Lincoln's Comment

Sir, please accept this as a testament to your love of poetry and an expression of my wishes for your peace of mind and heart. EKS

A thing of beauty is a joy for ever:
Its loveliness increases; it will never
Pass into nothingness; but still will ke
A bower quiet for us, and a sleep
Full of sweet dreams, and health, and
Therefore, on every morrow, are we wre
A flowery band to bind us to the earth,
Spite of despondence, of the inhuman d
Of noble natures, of the gloomy days,
Of all the unhealthy and o'er-darkene
Made for our searching: yes, in spite of a
Some shape of beauty moves away the
From our dark spirits.

Dear Aunt Emma,
Joy is the memory of things beautiful. Sorrow comes to all, and Death haunts us, but beauty will not pass away. Why is that? Because in the mind where memory lives, every rose-tinged sunrise still resides. Every field of goldenrod forever waves in an eternal breeze. Nothing is lost. Nothing is truly lost. Memory is a world mid-way between heaven and earth. This "flowery band" I have woven binds my heart to the Kentucky of my birth, and beauty does in fact move the pall from my dark spirits. How grateful I am for the enduring light of friendship.

A. Lincoln

AUTHOR'S NOTE

Readers who enjoy historical fiction generally accept that parts of a such a story will draw on actual people, places, and events, while much will be purely imagined. Some may be surprised by the central coincidences that underlie this story of a Keats-Lincoln connection. Now to separate fact from fiction.

THE SETTING

Hagan's Crossing is a fictional town located in an actual place, Oldham County, Kentucky, which is northeast of Louisville, bordering the Ohio River. The small town of Westport, Kentucky, occupies the spot on the map where I have placed Hagan's Crossing. Louisville, the largest city in Kentucky, is the site of the Kentucky Shakespeare Festival, where summer performances staged in the Central Park amphitheater draw large crowds. To my knowledge, no one has (literally) died on its stage.

FARMINGTON HISTORIC PLANTATION

Farmington Historic Plantation, now an 18-acre site, has restored the main house, the springhouse, and the barn and established a visitors' center which highlights the connections between the Speed family and the 16th president. Much work has been done to research the history of enslavement there, and a memorial to the more than 60 enslaved Africans who built and ran the plantation sits near the entrance. The 14-room house, designed with the influence of Thomas Jefferson, features original portraits and furnishings. With 550 acres, Farmington was a sizable working farm. Crops included hemp, corn, hay, wheat, potatoes, beans, peas, apples, and peaches, plus herds of milk cows, cattle, turkeys, chickens, and ducks. It stayed in the Speed family until Peachy Speed sold it to the Drescher family in 1865. Most of the acreage has been transformed into suburban neighborhoods.

The second Speed plantation, Endymion, is fictional. In actuality, after leaving Farmington, Philip and Emma Speed lived and raised their family in Louisville.

Farmington opened as a museum in 1959. Its mission has evolved over the years to present an honest interpretation of the life of the Speed family during the period 1816 to 1841.

Farmington was literally built by enslaved African Americans and sustained by their manual labor. As many as 70 enslaved men, women, and children lived there until 1865. While the interior of the main house has been painstakingly restored with authentic period furnishings, the programming presented by its owners, Historic Homes Foundation, Inc., emphasizes the role of slavery and the connection between Joshua Fry Speed and Abraham Lincoln over the beauty of the house. Working with the descendants of David and Martha Spencer and Abram and Rosanna Hayes—all of whom were enslaved at Farmington—and partnering with The Slave Dwelling Project, the management of Farmington hopes to continue to tell the authentic story of the Speed family and the people they enslaved.

LOUISVILLE AND THE SPEED FAMILY

Louisville, situated at the Falls of the Ohio, is Kentucky's largest city, widely known for the Kentucky Derby. The details "discovered" in the documents about the relationship of Meriwether Lewis Clark Jr., the grandson of explorer William Clark, and the members of the Churchill family are true. He was also the grandnephew of the city's founder, George Rogers Clark. The younger Clark was the child of Abigail Prather Churchill; it was her two brothers who provided the land for the famous Louisville racetrack. In the company of his wealthy Churchill uncles, Clark was inspired by British racing to establish the Derby.

The Speed family in America has many illustrious branches and famous individuals in its genealogy. Some of its members are descended from the 16th-century historian and cartographer John Speed. Captain James Speed, another well-known forebear, was born in Virginia and served in the Revolutionary War before traveling the Wilderness Road to Kentucky, where he settled near Danville. James's son John married Lucy Gilmer Fry and became a judge. John and Lucy Speed raised 11 children at Farmington, the home they built on Beargrass Creek, then eight miles south of the city of Louisville. Their children included Joshua Fry Speed, best remembered for his friendship with Abraham Lincoln; James Speed, whom Lincoln appointed attorney general in 1864; and Philip Speed, who married the daughter of George Keats, brother of the English Romantic poet.

Joshua Speed and Lincoln forged a close alliance in their young adulthood in Springfield, Illinois, when Speed shared a room above his mercantile store with the struggling lawyer.

Lincoln's three-week visit to Farmington, occasioned by

his serious depression, did occur in the summer of 1841, and Lincoln found it rejuvenating.

Members of the Speed family served in the military and in government posts and intermarried with other prominent Kentucky families, strongly influencing the growth of business and patronage of the arts. The J. B. Speed Art Museum, the University of Louisville Speed School of Engineering, and the Hattie Bishop Speed music collection, also at UofL, are a few examples of the family's legacy.

THE KEATS-SPEED CONNECTION

It is also true that newly wedded Philip Speed and Emma Keats Speed were living at Farmington and that in writing a letter to Mary Speed later in the year, Lincoln sent compliments to "Aunt Emma." That Emma Keats Speed met Abraham Lincoln is certain; her having given him a copy of the opening lines of *Endymion* is fantasy.

Likewise, it is true that George Keats, brother of the English Romantic poet John Keats, settled in Louisville in 1819, where he became a prominent citizen between 1821 and his death in 1841. He formed a cultural society that evolved into the Louisville Lyceum and ultimately into the University of Louisville. George bequeathed to daughter Emma his collection of letters and the handwritten poems of his brother John, who had died in Rome from tuberculosis in 1821, aged only 25.

Also true is the fragment of the letter from Oscar Wilde to Emma Keats Speed, thanking her for giving him Keats's original "Sonnet on Blue." Wilde was on a lecture tour in Louisville in 1882 when he praised the poem, not knowing until the end of the evening that Emma Keats Speed was in the audience. She approached him, inviting him to visit her the next afternoon, when she gave him the poem. In 1885, Wilde decried the rowdy auction of a batch of Keats's ephemera, not knowing that only ten years later, when he was imprisoned, his own poetry—and the framed copy of "Sonnet on Blue"—would be auctioned as well. The poem, now lost, was sold for 38 shillings, the equivalent of about $228 today. In contrast, a fragment of a Keats manuscript of the poem "I Stood Tiptoe" sold in 2013 for over $250,000!

SECOND SIGHT

In pre-Christian Celtic traditions, *an da shealladh*, meaning "two sights," describes the hereditary gift of being able to see beyond the boundaries of space and time. Among the Celts of the Scottish Highlands, belief in second sight was very strong; it also has a long history in Ireland. The Old Irish term *imbas* denotes the "vision that illumines," a sudden knowing or a vision of events that are remote in time or space.

The Irish folk hero Fionn MacCumhaill—anglicized as Finn McCool—was a poet-seer- hunter-warrior whose extrasensory gifts were legendary. Francine Nicholson's "The Sight, Gift of Celtic Seers," in *Land, Sea and Sky*, explains that people with this inherited gift are sensitive to "thin places" where the veil between this world and the eternal world is lifted and there are no boundaries within time and space.

Maggie O'Malley's inheritance of the second sight from her grandmother Nora very simply means that people from the past often show themselves to her, particularly when a mystery needs to be solved.

Sources of Chapter Titles

Chapter 1	Murder Most Foul	*Hamlet*
Chapter 2	The Rest is Silence	*Hamlet*
Chapter 3	What's Done is Done	*Macbeth*
Chapter 4	And Thereby Hangs a Tale	*Othello*
Chapter 5	Writ in Remembrance	*Richard II*
Chapter 6	And Nothing Is But What is Not	*Macbeth*
Genealogy of Franny Babcock		
Chapter 7	More Matter with Less Art	*Hamlet*
Chapter 8	Dreadful Note of Preparation	*Henry V*
Chapter 9	The Mind's Construction in the Face	*Macbeth*
Chapter 10	A Local Habitation and a Name	*A Midsummer Night's Dream*
Chapter 11	What's Past is Prologue	*The Tempest*
Chapter 12	The Evil That Men Do	*Julius Caesar*

Chapter 26	The Acting of a Dreadful Thing	*Julius Caesar*
Chapter 27	Give Sorrow Words	*Macbeth*
Chapter 28	This Fell Sergeant, Death	*Hamlet*
Chapter 29	It Ends a Mortal Woe	*Richard II*
Chapter 30	We Are Time's Subjects	*Henry IV, Part II*
Chapter 31	Speak Less than Thou Knowest	*King Lear*
Chapter 32	Life's Fitful Fever	*Macbeth*
Chapter 33	Rounded With a Sleep	*The Tempest*
Chapter 34	Time Shall Unfold	*King Lear*
Chapter 35	What Plighted Cunning Hides	*King Lear*
Chapter 36	The Be-All and the End-All	*Macbeth*

Made in the USA
Coppell, TX
17 December 2021